THE CHRISTMAS VISITOR

Rich man's daughter Eleanor is horrified when her father invites disgraced nobleman Rupert to join the family Christmas house party. But when the pair meet by accident, she finds him attractive, then is dismayed to learn his identity. Rupert and his valet fit in well, while gentle scheming by the indispensable Mr Steadman enhances Eleanor and Rupert's dawning relationship. Upstairs and downstairs, romance blossoms — but can both his lordship and his valet make amends for their past mistakes?

JILL BARRY

THE CHRISTMAS VISITOR

Complete and Unabridged

LINFORD
Leicester

First published in Great Britain in 2019

First Linford Edition
published 2020

A catalogue record for this book is available
from the British Library.

ISBN 978–1–4448–4613–3

Published by
Ulverscroft Limited
Anstey, Leicestershire

Set by Words & Graphics Ltd.
Anstey, Leicestershire
Printed and bound in Great Britain by
TJ Books Limited, Padstow, Cornwall

This book is printed on acid-free paper

Cloud on the Horizon

Sunshine still bathed the ancient stone manor house as the Honourable Eleanor Lansdown rode her chestnut mare back into her father's stable yard. The sound of Stella's hooves brought a young stable lad from the tack room to meet her.

'Thank you, Tommy.' Eleanor dismounted while the lad kept hold of her horse's bridle. 'Stella was in good form. Sailed over that drystone wall there!'

'Best not mention that to anyone else, Miss Eleanor. If you don't mind my saying.' Tommy's cheeks reddened.

'If I had to choose between talking about horses with you and the other lads, or making polite conversation with boring young gentlemen, I'm sure you know which I'd prefer!'

Tommy held the horse steady as Eleanor dismounted.

'If you can manage to slip away for a ride tomorrow, miss, it'd be appreciated. Fred's got the day off for his sister's wedding.'

'How lovely! Though that means you'll be one man short in the yard.'

'Don't you worry, Miss Eleanor, we'll cope all right, you see if we don't.'

'Ah, but Tommy, you've given me the perfect excuse to escape outdoors. I'd much prefer mucking out Stella's stable than joining in the drawing-room chit-chat,' she called over her shoulder as she made her way across the yard towards the house. 'Until tomorrow, then.'

★ ★ ★

Sophie Lansdown glanced up from her glossy magazine as her daughter entered her sitting-room.

'My dear, I'm so glad to see you back safe and sound — and with roses in your cheeks.'

'I've been putting Stella through her

2

paces, Ma, not attempting to scale Mount Everest. Surely I'm not late if Pa's not here yet?'

Her mother picked up her sherry glass.

'Your father's detained in town so it's only you and me today.'

'Pa's lying low at the office, is he? He always tries to keep out of the way on the run-up to Christmas.'

'As it happens, he has telephoned me with some very exciting news.'

Eleanor had soon realised her mother's mind was elsewhere. Why else would she not be insisting upon her daughter going straight upstairs to change from her riding clothes?

'Very interesting news, as it happens,' Sophie said.

Eleanor's lips twitched.

'Let me guess. I know! Amelia Earhart plans to land her aeroplane in the top field and spend Christmas with us!'

'Better than that, I fancy.'

Eleanor opened her mouth to protest

but saw her mother could hold back no longer.

'Your dear father has invited the Viscount Rupert Colford to stay with us for the Christmas celebrations.'

'Never heard of the old buffer.' Eleanor perched on a footstool. 'If he's not one of Pa's hunting cronies, how does he know this person well enough to invite him to stay?'

'He doesn't, dear. An old friend from your father's school-days has begged a favour on behalf of this gentleman.'

'The Viscount Colford and his fiancée were originally intending to spend the holiday at his family's estate near Bath, but circumstances have changed. Drastically, one might say.'

'How so?' Eleanor smothered a yawn.

Her mother leaned forward.

'Lord Colford has broken off his engagement, that's why. Understandably, his parents are none too pleased. He has plenty of friends in Somerset and London, but the poor young man

is anxious not to cause any embarrassment to them by turning up while he
remains under a cloud.'

Eleanor's eyebrows rocketed.

'Poor young man indeed! Whatever is
Pa thinking of, expecting us to put up
with this apology for a lord?'

'We don't know the full story,
Eleanor. The viscount's mother is
extremely upset and his father has
recommended he try to stay out of the
way until the scandal dies down. Your
own dear father says he's pleased to
help.' She shrugged. 'Every cloud has a
silver lining, you know.'

'I can't imagine why this particular
cloud should have one. If my arithmetic
is correct, that'll make thirteen of us at
table on Christmas Day.'

'I didn't realise you were so
superstitious, Eleanor! Imagine all the
wagging tongues if this young man
should venture out among friends and
family of his former fiancée and
himself.

'While he's staying here with us in

Wiltshire, he can keep out of the limelight.'

'I still think it's a rotten trick to play on that poor girl, especially so close to Christmas. Why can't the silly man take a suite of rooms in a hotel somewhere and lie low there? Instead, he's gate-crashing a private party of respectable people who are all strangers to him anyway.'

Her mother glanced at her gold wrist watch and coughed delicately.

'You really should go and change now, dear. All I can say about the viscount is that he is once again one of the most eligible bachelors in the West of England.'

'So what?'

'I sometimes wonder why your father spent all that money on finishing school fees!'

Eleanor got to her feet. She felt her heart bump in dismay because she might have known there'd be something more than sympathy behind her mother's agreement to this intrusion during the festive season.

'After lunch, we must see to some changes. His lordship must have the blue guest bedroom, which means Celia and Henry can go in the white room this year.'

Eleanor's hand was on the doorknob.

'What! Even if there are two of them and only one viscount?'

'We must afford his lordship the best possible hospitality. Surely you realise what a chance this is?'

Eleanor's worst fear was out of the cage and sneering.

'Don't talk such piffle, Mother!'

'Please don't speak to me like that, Eleanor. You have two minutes in which to change into a frock and join me in the dining-room.'

'All right, I apologise. But I want you to know matchmaking is not an option. You may consider this man a good catch, but don't expect me to flutter my eyelashes at him.

'Nobleman he may be, but your thirteenth person at table sounds like a complete cad and, if you place me beside him for Christmas dinner, I'll jolly well take my meal into the kitchen and eat with the staff. That'd probably be far more fun, anyway!'

'All right, darling.'

Eleanor glared in vain. Her mother's thoughts were already elsewhere.

'On your way, you might ask Violet to make up the spare bed in the footman's room. His lordship will be bringing his valet with him but I'm afraid those two will have to share that room for a few nights.'

'I might've known that man would be a nuisance. What a fuss!'

'It's only to be expected of a gentleman of his rank. The valet will assist our staff where necessary and that can only be an asset. Jeffers will remain in total charge, of course.'

* * *

Mrs Lizzie Potter ruled her culinary domain with help from her daughter,

8

Emmie, plus Violet, a young woman who walked from the village each morning and was collected at the end of the day by her father, who also worked on the Lansdown estate.

The annual festive house party required extra pairs of hands, though Mrs Potter had been known to insist she was better off with those used to working with her.

While the cook, white apron tied tightly around her neat figure, slid fillets of sole on to a silver serving dish, Violet added butter pats to the tureen of boiled potatoes and carrots.

'Good job the viscount is bringing his valet,' Mrs Potter said. 'As it is, with Mr Jeffers and the footman putting up decorations, you'll need to serve luncheon today, Violet. It's only the two ladies as his lordship's in town.'

Violet straightened up.

'Will the viscount's man be working with us then? Won't he think himself above that?'

'I'm told the valet will assist wherever

Mr Jeffers needs him. Lord Colford is expected tomorrow, in time for afternoon tea. Ooh, don't let me forget to put that tray of shortbread in the oven later.'

'Maybe the valet will be really handsome. Oops!' Violet knocked a carrot on the floor as she picked up the silver tureen of vegetables.

'Watch what you're about, my girl! No — don't put that one back in the dish.' Lizzie Potter shook her head. 'What'll I do with you, eh?'

'Sorry, Cook.'

Lizzie shrugged.

'Don't mind me. With so much to do, we all need to work together and that's a fact.

'You can ring the bell and take that food through now, Violet, there's a good girl. The lemon mousse is already on the sideboard and Madam says they'll serve themselves so you don't need to wait.'

She watched Violet load the tray and went ahead to open the door for her before turning her attention elsewhere.

'How are you doing with those marzipan fruits, Emmie?'

Her daughter looked up.

'Come and see what you think.'

The cook peered at the latest batch. Plump rosy strawberries frosted with powdered sugar, their leaves and stalk formed from green marzipan.

'I think you've quite a talent there, my girl. Maybe you should be training as a pastry cook?' She shot a thoughtful look at Emmie.

'I'm really enjoying this, Mum — I mean Cook. Desserts and sweetmeats are my favourite things to work on.'

'That's a good job, seeing as how you'll be whipping a dozen egg whites for the meringues, after lunch.' She winked at her daughter and turned around as Violet came back in, to address them both, her hands on her hips.

'Now, listen to me, you two. The next few days will be a tough row to hoe. You're both good workers but you'll need all your wits about you, so no skiving off to chatter with the stable lads.

'And if you happen to come across the guest of honour, don't go staring at him. I don't care if he looks like Rudolph Valentino or the back of an omnibus! In fact, it'd be a relief to find he's old enough to be your father.'

'What about Mr George?' Emmie asked.

'What about Mr George?'

'Violet's not met him yet. He was off skiing somewhere so he didn't come home last Christmas when she joined us.'

Lizzie Potter lifted her chin.

'I should hope that young man's corners have been rubbed off since working in London. His elder brother was never a nuisance like Master George.'

'George is handsome, though. He looks like I think Heathcliff might've looked,' Emmie said.

Violet smothered a giggle as she saw

Cook's expression.

'I encourage you to read books to improve your vocabulary, not to get you day-dreaming, my girl. Master George is a born flirt so don't either of you two forget it. As for you, Violet, I thought you'd begun walking out with the blacksmith's son?'

Violet's winter-pale cheeks suddenly rivalled the deep pink strawberry sweetmeats.

'He hasn't long asked me, Cook. Anyway, no harm in a girl looking, is there? It's only a bit of fun.'

'Hmm, you could do far worse than that young man, you know. Same as I warned you about the viscount, keep your eyes away from the both of 'em and always remember your situation. They belong in one place and we belong in another one. We should never forget it.'

'He'd never look at the likes of me anyway. Even I'm not daft enough to think that might happen.'

The older woman shook her head.

'You've a pretty face, is all I'm saying. Don't go letting him talk you into riding in that noisy motor car of his.'

Violet giggled.

'As if he'd do that! He must know there'll be girls all over him at the Boxing Night party.'

'Remember what I always say to Emmie. There's girls who know how to behave and there's girls who don't. And that holds good whether they're born with a silver spoon in their mouths, or not.'

'Which is best, d'you reckon?'

Cook fixed Violet with one of her looks.

'You mean class or wealth? All I can tell you is they don't always go hand in hand.' She lowered her voice. 'I shouldn't be talking like this to you, but you two girls know better than to gossip about the family.'

''Course we do,' Emmie said.

'This family is rolling in money. But they're what Mr Jeffers calls 'noovoh rich.' They mix with the upper class and entertain them like there's no tomorrow. But that young lord that's coming to stay, had better watch out for himself, if you ask me.'

'Why, Cook? I don't get it.'

Emmie looked pityingly at Violet.

'What she means is Mr and Mrs Lansdown will be looking to Miss Eleanor to marry into the upper class one day and raise their ... social standing. Isn't that right, Mum?'

Lizzie Potter nodded, for once not scolding her daughter for calling her Mum while at work.

'It could be an interesting few days. Now, Violet, you can call Mr Jeffers and the footman for their luncheon but don't you go letting on what we've been talking about. If you do, I'll have your guts for garters and that's a promise.'

Tantalising Image

'I thought we'd stop for a spot of luncheon in Devizes, Steadman.' The Viscount Colford glanced sideways at his valet.

'Very good, my lord.'

'You're welcome to take the wheel afterwards. I know you can't wait to get your hands on this motor. I can't understand why some chaps employ a chauffeur when driving's such a delight.'

Rupert felt at home behind the wheel of his gleaming Bentley, but he knew Alfred Steadman, who'd been his valet since the viscount graduated from Oxford University and took a position in his uncle's London law firm, also drove with skill.

'It will be my pleasure, sir,' Steadman said. 'I took the liberty of checking the mileage from Devizes to Starminster and if my calculations are correct, it's a little under twenty.'

'Good show.' Rupert bit his lip. 'We should reach the manor house well in time for tea. Except I can't say I'm looking forward to this house party, you know. Not one little bit, in fact. Mind you, it's jolly good of Edward Lansdown to take us in. It was out of the question for me to remain at home, given my mother's reaction to these shenanigans, but I jolly well wish we could have stayed put.'

'Understandable to feel like that, sir, if I may say so.'

'You certainly may, Steadman. I don't know how I'd have coped these last few days, without you taking most of the flak.'

'All part of the job, sir. At least no-one discovered your whereabouts.'

'Indeed. And what a relief that was. Claridge's is a tiptop hotel but I couldn't believe how many folk there were around who might have recognised me during our stay.

'That was a real brainwave of yours, lending me one of your outfits so I could sneak out for a breath of air. I've never been so delighted to set foot in Hyde Park!'

'I'm pleased to have been of assistance. The gentlemen of the Press can be a confounded nuisance at times, sir.'

Rupert heaved a sigh, as the road took them past fields where sheep grazed contentedly. He spotted one black sheep and smiled to himself at the thought of what he had in common with the animal.

'I really can't work out why I've suddenly become an object of such interest,' he said. 'A broken engagement is hardly the stuff of high drama, is it? It's not something of national importance, after all.'

'With respect, you do have a certain social standing, my lord. And your, er, former fiancée does have that royal connection.'

'I suppose so, though Velma's cousin twice removed or whatever it is, comes

18

from Austrian royalty and he hangs around with a crowd of titled folk I'd rather not think about, let alone socialise with.'

'I'd venture to say it's all the more important you escape the limelight and hope some other news item captures everyone's attention.'

'I don't miss her, you know. Velma, I mean. I think it's probably all for the best, putting a stop to things, don't you? For the life of me, I can't understand how I ever became involved with such a flibbertigibbet! If only folk knew her true character . . . '

Steadman cleared his throat.

'We're approaching the town out-skirts now, sir. Are you still thinking of stopping at the Bear Hotel for lun-cheon?'

'Oh, yes, definitely we will. Back in my school-days, my godfather used to take me there on occasions when we were allowed out. On the way, I remember him pointing out a white horse cut from the chalky hillside.'

'It sounds fascinating, sir.'

'Indeed. I was only thirteen at the time but I recall the Bear's food was excellent. It's an old coaching inn and I guarantee there'll be a roaring log fire to welcome us.' He glanced at his valet. 'You'll take your lunch with me in the dining-room, of course.'

'Thank you all the same, my lord, but I can eat elsewhere.'

'Nonsense, Steadman. While we're in limbo, so to speak, you're my companion and that's an end to it. You should know by now how I dislike eating alone in public.'

'Whatever you wish, sir. I trust my apparel will be appropriate.'

'I doubt anyone could distinguish which one of us was the valet and which the viscount. To be honest, I get more sense out of you than I do from most of the fellows I mix with.

'While we eat, you can clue me up about the Lansdown household. All I know is, apart from being worth an absolute fortune, Edward is well-known in the racing world. There's a local hunt, according to my father, but whether they'll rustle up a mount for me on Boxing Day is another matter.'

★   ★   ★

Eleanor stroked her horse's mane as the mare trotted on. She had stood by while her mother fussed over an already immaculate guest bedroom before deciding to slip away with the excuse of needing to purchase postage stamps.

The stamps would be useful for sending thank-you letters, but also provided an opportunity for Stella to gain a little more experience of the open road, with the possibility of meeting mechanical monsters on four wheels, rather than four legs.

Her expedition went without mishap and horse and rider were within sight of the manor house's ornate wrought-iron gateway when a starling plummeted from above and landed upon Stella's shapely head.

Eleanor gasped in horror, watched the dead bird topple to the ground then tried to calm the jittery horse.

'It's all right, Stella! The poor creature can't hurt you now. Steady . . . steady now.'

But the hasty response, intended to soothe, couldn't prevent the mare from rearing, casting Eleanor aside and on to the ground, like a hat swept away by the breeze. The horse trotted a few yards back along the road and came to a standstill.

Eleanor, feeling dazed, was still lying on the grass verge. She managed to prop herself up on one elbow, only to see Stella turn her head and swish her tail, as if unsure what to do next, as a red Bentley rounded the bend.

'Good heavens, what on earth's going on here?' In the passenger seat, the young viscount shaded his eyes against the last rays of December afternoon sunshine. 'Oh, gracious me, looks like the rider's been thrown!'

'I'll pull over, sir,' his valet said.

'Good job, Steadman. Leave the horse to me while you check on the rider. Whatever you do, don't mention my name. In fact, better not call me anything at all if you can wangle it.'

The older man halted the vehicle and Rupert, discarding the woollen rug he'd tucked around his legs, opened the passenger door and climbed over the running board. The chestnut eyed him warily as he moved but held her ground. Rupert kept his gaze locked upon the horse's eyes and continued to walk slowly forward.

'There, there, girl. Nothing to fear.' He murmured more soothing words and, once close enough, raised his hand slowly to the mare's nostrils. The animal didn't protest, so, heartened, Rupert gave her nose a rub. She whickered softly.

'Good girl.' Rupert took hold of the reins. A swift glance revealed his valet crouched beside the motionless figure of the rider at the roadside.

Rupert began to lead the mare slowly along the highway towards Steadman and the person now sitting upright on the grass verge. The valet appeared to be examining this person's left foot. A discarded riding boot lay beside someone who Rupert now realised was an extremely attractive young lady.

At once he pictured Velma, she who had beguiled him with her violet eyes and corn silk hair. He'd been bemused by her kittenish looks, her feminine wiles and honeyed tones, not to mention her glamorous royal connections. What a fool he had been!

She'd betrayed him while he was out of town on business. By chance, she and an older man about town had been spotted in a secluded hotel where by chance, a close friend of Rupert's had been dining with his wife.

It didn't matter that Velma protested she'd been bored and lonely without her darling fiancé so had accepted an invitation to dinner. What harm could there possibly be in that? She had fluttered her eyelashes at Rupert but the damage was done and he knew he could no longer trust her to be a loyal and faithful wife.

Ever the gentleman, as some of his friends commented, while shaking their heads in sympathy, Rupert chose to bear the blame for ending his short-lived engagement to the Honourable Velma.

He felt it was the chivalrous thing to do, but only his closest friends knew the truth and understood his relief at having avoided marriage to someone so flighty.

But now, away from his London life and standing on a country road in deepest Wiltshire, he found himself once more in danger of allowing his heart to rule his head. But he must curb dangerous romantic thoughts involving an unknown beauty with melting brown eyes and a complexion like peaches and cream.

Society saw him as a cad and his offer to save Velma's reputation had placed him in a position where he daren't look at girls in any other way but as fellow human beings. And he certainly didn't feel inclined to introduce himself to the young lady who seemed totally comfortable to have his valet holding her hand between his own. Hmm.

Rupert drew himself up to his full height.

'Good afternoon, ma'am. I trust you're not in too much pain. You'll be pleased to hear your horse appears unharmed.'

'The young lady has, I believe, sprained her ankle,' Steadman said. 'I've suggested we give her a lift to her home.'

Good old Steadman, Rupert thought. One could always rely on him. He smiled down at the injured girl.

'We'll be pleased to take you home. How far away do you live, Miss, er . . . ?'

'Eleanor Lansdown.' She held out her gloved right hand. 'How do you do?

We live at Starminster Manor, just up the road there, so I almost made it home in one piece. Thank goodness Stella's not hurt, though.'

Whilst reeling from the shock of knowing he was in the company of his host's daughter, Rupert warmed to her immediately. Velma would have been screaming like a banshee and already planning to sell the horse because of course the animal would have been to blame. He pulled himself together.

'I take it the gateway I can see is where you mean?'

'It is.' Eleanor lifted her chin and smiled at him. 'But what about my horse?' She flexed the injured foot and winced. 'No. I certainly daren't ride her back. Oh, dear.'

Rupert gulped and cast his valet what he knew must be a desperate glance.

'With your permission, Miss Lansdown, I shall lead your horse home while Mr Steadman drives you to your door. I'm quite used to horses so don't worry about her. What's her name?'

'Stella. She's my guiding star.'

Rupert patted Stella's head and the horse nuzzled his arm.

Eleanor smiled up at Rupert and let go of Alfred Steadman's reassuring hand.

'That's so very civil of you. What amazing luck the two of you came along when you did!'

Her low, beautiful voice and radiant smile, even while in such an uncomfortable position, would have brightened even the gloomiest of days.

'Allow me to lift you up and get you into the car,' the viscount said.

'Ah, I'm not so good with horses as you are, my . . . erm . . . my friend. Perhaps the young lady will permit me to lift her? I'm sure she's as light as a feather.'

Rupert stood by, keeping Stella company, while his valet hoisted the beautiful invalid up from the grass verge, steadying her as she stood upright before taking a cautious step on to the road.

The valet frowned.

'I think it's safer if I carry you to the car, Miss Lansdown.'

'All right, Mr Steadman. I'm sorry for being such a nuisance.' She glanced at Rupert. 'I'll direct you to the stables once we're on the driveway. Do you gentlemen live in this part of the world? I don't recall meeting either of you before.' She looked from one to the other.

'Perhaps my mother and I could offer some refreshment before you continue your journey?'

The viscount and his valet exchanged glances. Neither spoke. This young lady's manners were impeccable as one would expect. And Rupert suddenly realised how impolite he must seem and how ridiculous it would be to continue his pathetic attempt to conceal his identity.

They could hardly accompany Miss Lansdown back to the house where they were invited to join in the Christmas festivities without confessing their reason for being in the vicinity.

'Please forgive my rudeness. I don't know what I was thinking of. I'd like to introduce myself as Rupert Colford and this gentleman is Alfred Steadman, my trusted valet and companion.' He held out his hand a second time. 'I imagine you know that we're to be guests of your parents?'

Eleanor extended her hand, very slowly, and, he realised, with much reluctance.

'You mean you are the viscount who — ' Rupert nodded.

'Who is fortunate enough to be joining your house party, Miss Lansdown.'

She nodded.

'Would you be kind enough to assist me to the car, Mr Steadman?'

'Perhaps I should bring the car closer, Miss Lansdown?' Steadman was still supporting Eleanor.

'That would be most kind, Mr Steadman.'

'Top idea,' Rupert said. 'I'll wait here

with Miss Lansdown and Stella.' He held out his free arm. While he thought Eleanor looked as though she'd been asked to hold paws with a mountain bear, she slipped her hand in the crook of his arm, allowing him a drift of a light, floral perfume.

Eleanor was watching Steadman sprint back to the Bentley.

'What a thoroughly nice chap he is,' she said. But her warm tone soon chilled. 'Maybe I should try riding back after all. These jodhpurs are decidedly damp and I'd hate to cause any damage to your car's upholstery, Lord Colford.'

He decided not to push his luck by insisting she called him by his first name.

'I couldn't care two hoots about a bit of damp, but shouldn't you have your ankle examined before getting back in the saddle, Miss Lansdown? For one thing, I don't believe that swelling will allow you to wear your riding boots.'

'How very annoying! If I have to sit around with my feet up, I'll be at the mercy of anyone looking to bore me with tedious tales of the play they saw in London last week.

'As for atrocities like whist and bridge, if I see anyone even opening a pack of playing cards, I'll pretend to be asleep! I should warn you, our vicar in particular is a demon.'

She looked up at Rupert. He knew she could see the mirth sparkling in his eyes. For moments, they gazed at one another while he fantasised about scooping her up in his arms and carrying her off, sprained ankle and all, in his motor car. Somewhere with no other people around would be wonderful.

This image so tantalised him, he couldn't bear to look away. Nor, apparently, could she. Until, perhaps remembering she was in the company of currently the most despised member of the British aristocracy, she turned her head and heaved a sigh.

Long-Lost Love

'This really is most inconsiderate of you, Eleanor.' Her mother had appeared in the doorway of her daughter's bedroom.

The glare Eleanor gave her should have turned her to stone.

'I didn't exactly plan to fall from my horse, Mother.'

'I meant it was inconsiderate to sneak off for a ride instead of changing into a pretty tea gown and playing the piano for Aunt Hester. You know how much she loves Christmas carols.' Sophie Lansdown settled herself on the window seat.

'How was I to know she'd arrive so early? It's not very good form, is it?'

'Hester is my elder sister, darling! Friends were kind enough to drop her off on their way to Bath. But worst of all is how close you came to causing a bad accident. Both you and his lordship might have been injured, as well as his man.'

Eleanor counted to ten. Silently.

'Where is the viscount, anyway?'

'Keeping Aunt Hester company in the drawing-room.'

Eleanor giggled.

'Divine retribution! She's probably telling him all about her trip to the Pyramids at the turn of the century. I could almost feel sorry for him. Almost,' she added.

'I really should go and join them. We can't have Lord Colford thinking I'm a bad hostess though Hester can of course be quite entertaining. Sometimes. It would be far easier if your father came home to help. After all, he's the one who invited that young man.'

'I'm sure Pa won't be long.' Eleanor spoke soothingly. 'Anyway, I don't need you to stand guard over me, Mother. Someone can show the doctor where I am when he arrives.'

'This isn't the best of starts to our Christmas.' Eleanor's mother got up and walked over to the door. 'But I'm very sorry if you're in pain, my dear.'

Eleanor turned her head away to hide a tear. Her mother and the staff would ensure the household was well fed and entertained. But she was absolutely right. A sprained ankle was highly inconvenient.

Eleanor had planned to visit the stables again early next morning, and muck out Stella's box, to help Tommy and his mates out. Life was so unfair sometimes.

She reached for her handkerchief as someone tapped on the sitting-room door.

'Come in.'

To her surprise, Alfred Steadman stood on the threshold.

'Excuse me, Miss Eleanor, but his lordship wishes to enquire about your health. I understand your mother is needed in several places at once so I took the liberty of calling upon you.'

She waved him in.

'I'm not at death's door, so do come and talk to me, Alfred. You don't mind if I call you Alfred?'

She watched his look of surprise.

'It's a little unusual, Miss Eleanor. Under the circumstances.'

'Nonsense! I'm fully dressed. You've carried me in your arms, placed a rug beneath my soggy jodhpurs and driven me home after my mishap, so why stand on ceremony?'

He looked delighted, she thought as he moved five paces inside the room, immaculate in his valet's neat attire. He was also, she thought, quite handsome for a man in his forties.

Although there was a kind of resignation about him, as though he was disappointed or sad about something. She hoped his master wasn't difficult to work for. Dreadful man!

'His lordship and I were pleased to help. No-one could have left you there without stopping to assist you.'

'It was rather a shock. Discovering

36

who my rescuer was, I mean.'

Alfred nodded.

'I do believe the feeling was mutual, Miss Eleanor.'

'Well, you may thank his lordship for his kind inquiry and inform him I'm still awaiting a visit from the family doctor. Until he informs me what I may or may not do, I might just as well be shipwrecked.'

'If I make so bold, Miss Eleanor, if you have anything with which I can assist you, I shall of course not hesitate to come to your aid.'

'You really are a sweet man, Alfred.' She saw his surprised expression. 'I mean it, you know. You're not at all like certain people I could mention.'

'Anyone would have done the same as his lordship and me, miss.'

'Well, you're very kind to offer further assistance, but the main thing bothering me is Stella. If I can't get out to visit her, let alone ride her to the Boxing Day Meet, I shall be heartbroken.'

'I'm no horseman, I'm afraid. Perhaps his lordship . . . ?'

She shook her head.

'I shouldn't look on the black side, but I suspect I'll be forced to sit around for the time being. There is something I can do, though — something to repay you for your kindness.'

Alfred bowed his head.

'With respect, Miss Eleanor, it's not necessary. You have enough to concern you.'

She looked up at him.

'Ah, but it's occurred to me that we shouldn't expect you to share a room with our footman. I understand you are as much a friend and companion as you are a valet to Lord Colford?'

'Please don't worry yourself on my account, miss.'

'But I insist! I can't do it myself, but I'll ensure my mother instructs someone to strip the linen from the original bed and take it to the old nursery.

'I think my mother must have forgotten that the bed our nanny used to sleep in is still in the little side room. You'll have privacy and probably a twinkly-eyed teddy bear or two for company.'

Someone pushed the door wide open.

'Our dear doctor is here, Eleanor.'

Before Mrs Lansdown could say another word, Alfred gave a slight bow in her direction and made his way out.

'Thanks for keeping me company,' the invalid called. She smiled sweetly at the family doctor. 'I do hope you'll be able to work some magic on me. It's very important I can get around and help my poor, overworked mother.'

★ ★ ★

Alfred Steadman recognised her as soon as he stepped inside the kitchen. When Mr Jeffers mentioned the cook was called Mrs Potter, the name had meant nothing. Even if he'd heard her name was Lizzie, it could well have been any old Lizzie. But fate had decreed she was, really was, his Lizzie.

She'd aged well. Probably better than he had, having suffered the trenches as lodgings for much of the Great War years.

He'd been one of the lucky ones. So many of his generation ended their lives in Flanders. Too many tears wept. He could do without sad memories. But seeing his former sweetheart had ruffled his normally steady emotions.

'More tea, Mr Steadman?'

'Ah, yes, please, Mr Jeffers.'

'You were miles away. I had to ask twice,' the butler said.

'I beg your pardon. I was thinking back to old times. Other kitchens I've sat in. You know the sort of thing.'

'I do indeed, and especially at Christmas time. This is one of the better households I've worked in and I see no reason to seek employment elsewhere.' He leaned forward.

'The family are typical nouveau riche, of course, but they try hard to fit into the kind of society to which you and I are well-accustomed.' He nodded towards the kitchen range. 'They've kitted the place out well. No expense spared, as I'm sure you'll have noticed.'

'Have you been with the family long?' Alfred spooned sugar into his teacup.

'I've been here for four years. Mrs Potter has been cook here much longer than that. Mr Lansdown and family inherited her when they purchased the manor house.'

He inclined his head towards the young girl piping whipped cream on a trifle.

'Emmie there's her daughter. She's a good girl, lucky too, having a mother who can train her up. Skilful cooks can always find a position. If she doesn't get her head turned by some lad, she could move to London. Get a job in a smart hotel like the Savoy or the Ritz.'

'She could indeed, if she shows promise.' Alfred shifted his position slightly. 'How about her, um, father? Might I enquire if Mr Potter works for the family, too?'

'Mrs Potter is a widow, poor soul. Her husband used to work on a local farm and I'm afraid he met a most unfortunate end. Not the most pleasant of subjects for a Christmas Eve, as I'm sure you'll understand.'

'Of course. Poor woman.'

Alfred glanced over his shoulder at the woman so engrossed with her cooking. He wondered if, beneath her cap, that red-gold hair, inherited by her daughter — who'd allowed a tendril to escape from beneath her own cap — still retained any of its former glory.

Lizzie Potter had taken not a blind bit of notice of him. Probably hadn't even seen him sit down in the alcove. Why would she, with all the responsibility she bore?

The girl called Violet had made them a pot of tea and Mr Jeffers reckoned it was pointless introducing him to the staff while they were preparing Christmas Eve supper. Would Lizzie even recognise him? Might his name spark a distant memory?

'Finished your tea? Come on, then.' Mr Jeffers got to his feet. 'You can meet us all properly when we sit down for our own supper.'

Alfred followed the butler, leaving behind simmering saucepans and appetising odours, to walk along the dimly lit corridor towards the stairs. At the top, Mr Jeffers pushed open the door to a very different domain.

As an experienced gentleman's valet, Alfred felt equally at home when walking upon luxurious carpets as he did on worn linoleum, but it occurred to him that he mightn't feel so relaxed later, coming face to face with someone who'd once meant so much to him.

He set off to locate the viscount.

$\star$ $\star$ $\star$

'Well, I'm blessed! Did she really say that thing about death's door? What a little minx the girl is.' Rupert peered at his reflection in the cheval mirror.

'If I might say so, my lord, Miss

Eleanor has many redeeming qualities. We enjoyed a most cordial discussion.'

'Really? I thought her main concern was her horse.'

'The young lady is obviously very devoted to Stella,' Alfred said.

'Quite so. I would hedge a bet she's fonder of that mare than she is of anyone else.'

Alfred cleared his throat.

'As for the household, the staff seem decent enough. Mr Jeffers is a regular sort of fellow and, as luck would have it, we follow the same football team.'

'I'm a great disappointment to you in that respect.'

'I think your tie needs a tweak, my lord. Allow me.'

'Thank you, Steadman. Ever the soul of tact.'

'As for the cook, I'm told Mrs Potter has years of experience in the kitchen.'

'Good show. If afternoon tea's anything to go by, we shall all be in for a treat this evening. I'm sure you'll be well fed, too.' The viscount checked his watch. 'My word, is that the time?'

'No rush, sir. In fact, I've promised Jeffers to help him carry Miss Eleanor downstairs. She can bear weight on her injured foot but the doctor recommends resting it as much as possible.'

'Gosh. How did she get upstairs in the first place?'

'Mr Jeffers and I were pleased to be of assistance.'

'Were you, by Jove?'

'There's something else I meant to say to you, sir . . .'

'While I think of it, I'm sorry you have to share a room, Steadman. Very glad you're here to keep an eye on me, though. Much appreciated and all that.'

'It is my job, sir. Life with you is never dull. Now, if I could just tell you . . .'

'Hmm. Nice of you and all that, but lately it's been mayhem. All that cloak and dagger business, dodging the Press. Total twaddle!'

'I know our stay isn't destined to be a lengthy one, but perhaps matters will have quietened down by the time we return to London.'

'Let's hope you're right. Our hostess has given me a jolly nice room and they seem pleasant enough, although I reckon Miss Eleanor regards me as lower than the lowliest earthworm.'

'So, what about your quarters? Hope they haven't slotted you in with a snorer. You must have had enough of that during the war, poor chap.'

'Indeed. But as it happens, my lord, I'm billeted down the corridor in . . . '

'Good show.' Rupert whirled around. 'You'd better get off then. I know you'll be a tremendous help over these next few days, Steadman, what with one thing and another. See you later, old chap.'

Ill-Timed Announcement

The lady of the house was either heeding her daughter's comment about seating plans or playing a wily game. At dinner, Eleanor found herself sitting between her younger brother, George, and her elder brother, Henry.

Unfortunately, the visiting viscount was seated opposite but Eleanor judged his neighbours would engage him in conversation and prevent him from peering round the centrepiece of bronze and white chrysanthemums and sprigs of holly screening each of them from the other.

'I only just made it,' George said, buttering a roll. 'Ma hardly bothered to ask after my health or my journey, she was so intent on telling me about our unexpected guest.'

Eleanor peered between two chrysanthemums and checked to make sure the viscount was deep in conversation with her sister-in-law.

'What did she say about him, Georgie?'

'Apart from reciting his illustrious pedigree? Only that he'd been let down last moment, forced to change his plans and Pa took pity on him. She must think I take no notice whatsoever of what goes on in London society.'

'The trouble is,' Eleanor said, 'she tends to borrow inspiration from Mrs Bennet in 'Pride And Prejudice'.'

'Mrs who?'

'It doesn't matter. Our mother is surveying the field for possible suitors.'

'For you?' George put down his soup spoon.

'No, you dunderhead — for my horse! Goodness me, Georgie, who else would she be fussing about?'

George chuckled.

'I keep thinking you're still in finishing school and interested only in four-legged creatures.'

'Well, they're generally more reliable

than men.' Eleanor's treacherous insides lurched as the viscount found humour in some quip of her aunt Hester's.

He possessed a laugh delicious enough to send tingles down the spine of a stone statue. His eyes sparkled with intelligence and kindliness. If he wasn't such a bounder, and if she was seeking a tall, handsome husband, which she certainly wasn't, she would have been more than a little interested in becoming better acquainted.

'According to Ma, the viscount's a lawyer, but being groomed to manage his father's Somerset estate,' George said. 'Rather him than me. I prefer working in the City to vegetating in the sticks.'

'So it would seem.' Eleanor turned to answer a question her elder brother was asking her.

'I'm rather surprised Ma's so eager to entertain him,' George muttered through the side of his mouth. 'Word is, he's not the most sought-after house guest just now, but I don't frequent his exalted circles, so really shouldn't comment on halfhearted rumour-mongering.'

'Our mother makes up her own mind. You should know that by now.'

George chuckled.

'You're absolutely right. Anyway, living in London isn't only about the social whirl, it's the feeling of being at the hub of things. You should come and visit, sis. I'm sure you'd soon find someone to marry you.'

'I have no wish to find a husband. I hated having to be presented at Court and going to all those stupid parties. Aunt Hester did her best, but I know I was a great disappointment to her.'

'Not as much as you are to Ma!'

'I wish people would understand I'm not on the lookout for a husband. I haven't done half the things I want to do yet, so let me make that absolutely clear.'

'Make what clear, little sister?' On her other side, Henry leaned closer.

'I was telling Georgie, no matter what our mother or anyone else may think, I'm not interested in potential suitors.' Eleanor's voice rang out loud and clear as the bubble of conversation dissolved at that precise and ill-timed moment.

Horrified, Eleanor watched the viscount's head appear around the edge of the seasonal greenery. While her mother chimed in with what she recognised as a desperate ploy to save face, by mentioning Midnight Mass at the nearby church, Lord Colford treated Eleanor to a mischievous wink. Had she been standing up, she'd have gone weak at the knees.

She lowered her gaze, praying she wouldn't blush, and wished she'd contracted an ailment, any ailment, as long as it kept her pinned to her room, unlike the sprained ankle that allowed her to join the party and blurt out unfortunate comments.

'Well, thanks for spelling that out.' Henry patted her hand. 'Bad luck about the ankle, Ellie. At least you've plenty of strong men to carry you around.'

'Alfred Steadman has helped Jeffers cart me up and downstairs. He really is a delightful gentleman.'

Henry looked puzzled.

'Who? I don't see him at the table.'

'Of course you don't. Mr Steadman is his lordship's valet, which means he's helping Jeffers below stairs.'

'I see. Well, that sounds a sensible arrangement. I'm looking forward to making the viscount's acquaintance later. He seems a friendly sort of chap,' Henry said.

Obviously, flappers' gossip hadn't penetrated the area of Bristol where Eleanor's eldest brother lived. Unsure how to avoid breaking the unsavoury news of the viscount's broken engagement, she fidgeted with her table napkin. Inspiration struck.

'I'm so cross I can't run around with the twins this year. It's very frustrating.'

'At least they have one another for company. And the young nanny's very good with them. What about reading to them or doing jigsaws instead?'

Eleanor grinned.

'It seems my role in life is already mapped out. I'm becoming the perfect spinster aunt and dutiful niece, rolled into one.'

'What rot!' Henry chuckled. 'Some dashing young fellow will snap you up before long, you mark my words. Millie thinks you've blossomed into a beauty while you've been away in Switzerland.'

'Did she really say that?'

'Oh, yes. Come to think of it, I'd wager you left more than one broken heart behind you in the Alps or wherever you were loafing around.'

'Not so loud, Henry. I don't want Mother suspecting anything.'

'Doesn't she realise what certain finishing schools are like?'

'Why would she? She's never set foot in one. She read all the brochures and believed every single word. Fortunately, Aunt Hester recommended the place I attended.'

'There's more to the old girl than meets the eye, don't you think?'

'All I know is that people conceal more secrets than one might imagine.'

'This smoked salmon is excellent.' Henry munched and swallowed. 'So, has brother George been telling you all his secrets?'

'Hardly.' She glanced sideways. 'At the moment, he's doing an excellent job of keeping Aunt Hester entertained.'

'Probably sweet-talking her into leaving all her fortune to him!'

Eleanor giggled.

'That's very naughty of you.'

'I know George only too well. So, tell me more about your Swiss adventure. Near Lake Geneva, wasn't it, if I recall correctly?'

'It was. Wonderful scenery, but there's not much to tell. I'm sure you know what boring subjects are taught in these places.'

'But there must have been a beau or two, surely?'

Eleanor took a deep breath.

'A girl I chummed up with had a boyfriend she met at someone's house. All very proper — friends of her parents, she said. I was invited to make up a four and go to a party.'

'What did your chaperones say to that?'

'They knew nothing. One of the girls promised to creep down and unbolt the back door for us.'

'Did all go well?'

'We got mildly squiffy, drinking champagne, but no-one found out. I enjoyed a little flirtation, shall we say?'

'Good for you. You should be having fun at your age.'

'The things we had to practise in our lessons could hardly be described as fun.'

'What did you dislike most?'

'Being taught how to enter and leave a motorcar without showing too much leg. How to address a bishop and all the usual dreary stuff.'

'How to undress a bishop?'

'Henry! Stop making me laugh. All I

need is to choke and ruin everyone's meal.'

'You won't do that. The food's always marvellous. Give Ma her due.'

'You mean she employs a talented cook?'

'Touché! I guess Mrs Potter's still here. What about her Emmie? She's always been good with the twins.'

'Both of them still with us, yes. You'd do well to make sure our brother doesn't pester Emmie to go out in his motor car as he did last Christmas.'

'Hasn't the young whippersnapper found someone to love yet? I must have a few words.'

Eleanor laid down her cutlery.

'Why is everyone so obsessed about finding love?'

She wished the floor would open up and swallow her. Across the table, Jeffers was leaning in to remove the centrepiece. Eleanor's last remark must have sounded as clear to everyone as church bells ringing on a frosty morning.

Everyone, including of course his most irritating highness, Lord Colford. Even if he did look disturbingly handsome in dinner jacket and black tie and making her dream of running her fingers through his hair. Maybe the wine had gone to her head.

Later, several family members set off on foot to the nearby church. Staff who wished to attend were encouraged to do so and Alfred Steadman, receiving permission from Lord Rupert, joined the small group gathering in the kitchen. Mr Jeffers led the way. Alfred brought up the rear.

There was no sign of Lizzie Potter but he decided he must somehow manage to get her on her own and see whether she remembered him. If he wasn't mistaken, she'd have put duty before her own wishes, and continued with her preparations for the next day.

He was pleased to see Emmie and Violet had opted to join the congregation and were well-wrapped up against the night air.

A sprinkling of stars twinkled against the dense dark sky. The air was still, though cold enough to make the walkers trot briskly towards the golden glow from the lights of St Peter's Church.

There was barely a seat left but Alfred found two spare places in one of the pews near the back and received whispered thanks from Emmie and Violet whom he knew had been on their feet most of the day.

He stood at the back with Mr Jeffers and a couple of men he hadn't met before.

Alfred was shocked to feel tears stinging as the choir began their procession down the aisle and the chosen choirboy sang the first line of 'Once in Royal David's City'.

This was one of his favourite hymns and he blinked back the tears, hoping nobody had noticed him, and joined in with his melodious baritone voice when the time came for the congregation to sing, too.

The smell of fresh green ivy and fir tree branches mingled with the scent of wax candles and incense, taking Alfred back to those days when he'd first noticed a girl with hair gleaming like the copper candlesticks his mother kept on the front parlour mantelpiece.

He'd found it difficult to take his eyes off her and she'd haunted his dreams for weeks before he plucked up courage to introduce himself to her after that evening's service ended and he was able to take her aside.

Alfred joined the queue of worshippers waiting to take Communion and sent up a little prayer for guidance. If Lizzie failed to remember him, should he back off and not dredge up old memories? Or, worse, if she should remember him, but wanted nothing further to do with him, should he try to convince her of his sincerity?

On the walk back, hands thrust in the pockets of his long overcoat, his heart told him what he must do.

Memories Rekindled

The object of his thoughts and prayers was the only person remaining in the kitchen when Alfred Steadman peered round the door, unable to go to his room before satisfying his curiosity.

'Hello, Lizzie,' he said. 'Who'd have thought we'd meet again after all these years?'

She made no reply, only beckoned him to sit down with her at the kitchen table.

He longed to put his arms around her. Now he'd found her again, he wanted to say so much to her. He pulled out the chair opposite hers and sat down.

'I wasn't sure you'd remember me,' he said.

'Typical man! I remember you very well, Alfred. I was wondering whether you'd show your face after you went to

Midnight Mass.'

He grinned, feeling about sixteen years of age again.

'You're looking in the pink, Mrs Potter, if you don't mind me saying.'

'You too, Mr Steadman. Rather dapper, I'd say, in your smart valet's outfit. I could hardly believe my eyes when I realised it was you. I almost dropped too much salt into the soup pan!'

'Well, good job you didn't. You keep a tidy ship here. My viscount's highly impressed with your cooking, Lizzie.'

'I couldn't believe the kind message he sent me after dinner. Mr Jeffers informed me how pleased he was. Sounds like he's a good employer?'

Alfred nodded.

'My employer is a man of the people. It was also Mr Jeffers who told me you'd been widowed. I'm very sorry to hear that. It couldn't have been easy for you, with a daughter to raise and all. Must say, I never thought you'd turn out to be such an accomplished cook.'

She raised her eyebrows.

'Why would you have? I worked in a hospital kitchen when we first met. Peeling vegetables mostly, back then. In a way it did me a service, because I was determined not to be a skivvy for too long.'

'I'm pleased you've a good position here. You've done well, Lizzie.'

'Thank you, but life's all about changes and never giving up, don't you think?'

He held her gaze.

'I need you to know I didn't want to give you up, after we got together. But I expect you remember I had the offer of the job in Canada. It's what I'd always dreamed of. Travel. New horizons. Especially after the war years.'

'I understand. I knew I could never compete with your dreams. But I missed you when you'd gone. You were so kind to me and my mother during the months we were going out together. She thought the world of you.'

'She was a lovely person. I let her

down, as I did you, Lizzie. I should've asked you to go to Quebec with me. I fell for you and I think you felt the same about me. We could have easily found you a position out there.'

'I couldn't have left home. Not even if you'd gone down on bended knee with a steamer ticket in one hand and a diamond ring in the other. My mother's health was failing and I'd never have slept easy at night had I deserted her.'

He saw within her the same loyalty and sweet nature that attracted him in that former life.

'How did she do? I'm sorry if I'm bringing back sad memories.'

'She hung on for a few months after my daughter was born. Not long after you left, I met my husband-to-be and he was very kind to my mum too. We married later in the year you went away and Emmie came along in December 1908. She was my Christmas blessing! You might remember Wilf Potter from when we all attended the same church?'

'I'm afraid not, but I'm glad you found a decent chap.' Alfred had no idea who she meant. His head must have been chock-a-block with Canadian dreams as well as his admiration for the trim young woman whose hair was bright as maple leaves in the Fall. But what a fool he'd been to let her go.

'At least Ma lived to see her granddaughter,' Lizzie said.

'I'm glad. Mr Jeffers told me how talented Emmie is.'

Lizzie's face lit up.

'He reckons she has it within her to go places. Find a position in a top hotel. Who'd have thought it?'

'I'm not surprised,' Alfred said, 'seeing who her mum is. I imagine Emmie speaks nicely too. As you always did.'

Lizzie got up and went over to a cupboard, reaching down a bottle of brandy from the top shelf.

'Purely medicinal. I think we've both had a big shock today.' She poured two measures into brandy goblets from a tray of glasses lined up like soldiers waiting for a spit and polish. 'It's not nicked from the wine cellar, in case you're wondering.'

'As if I'd think such a thing of you! Thank you,' he said, taking the glass she handed him. It seemed inappropriate to propose a toast to times gone by and he surprised himself when he noticed how his hand trembled. Emotions he'd kept buried for years were rocking his usual stability that night, and he wasn't sure how to cope.

'Happy Christmas,' Lizzie said as she raised her glass.

'And to you, my dear,' Alfred said.

Each of them took a sip of the golden liquid. He felt the powerful spirit slip down his throat. Warming. Relaxing. Welcome.

He put down his brandy goblet.

'I still feel insanely jealous of your late husband.' He saw Lizzie frown. 'I'm sorry, ridiculous it may be, but it's true.'

She looked down at the glass she

cradled in her hands.

'There's no going back, Alfred. And you wouldn't resent me having had my daughter, now would you?'

'Of course not! But you and me — we might've had a son and a daughter together.'

'Don't torture yourself with such thoughts.' Lizzie took another sip from her glass.

'When I came back to see my mother before I joined the Army, I called at your house, you know. But there were new folk living there and they had no idea where you'd gone.'

'Wilf and Emmie and me — we'd moved out here by then. There were jobs going in the house and on the estate, what with so many men being sent overseas. Wilf never joined up of course.

'He didn't pass the medical and, to my shame, I couldn't help but be relieved. I'd already lost you and I couldn't stand the thought of losing him as well.'

Alfred reached across the table and took her hand.

'He'd have been needed on the home front. He would've made himself useful, I wager.'

'He did. But he never stopped wishing he could've gone and done his bit out there. It ate away at him.' She paused. 'I hate war. I wish it didn't have to happen.'

Alfred squeezed her hand before releasing it.

'In an ideal world . . . '

'How long did you stay out in Canada?'

'Until I needed to come back and fight.'

She twirled the stem of her brandy goblet between her slim fingers.

'You must've had it rough out there, over in France?'

'I got out of it alive. You must have gone through plenty yourself, Lizzie. I used to think about you a lot when I was in the trenches. Wonder where you were. What you were doing. I didn't even have a photograph to tuck in my wallet.'

'We mustn't get maudlin.' She glanced at the big round clock on the wall. 'You know the story now. What's done is done and I need to be up before the birds tomorrow.' She drained her glass.

Alfred got up from his chair.

'I'm glad we had this chat. Thank you, Lizzie. Thank you for telling me your story.'

She walked with him towards the door.

'I have a room down here so I'll switch off the lights and get myself to bed. Goodnight, Alfred.'

He hesitated before dipping his head and kissing her on the cheek.

'Goodnight, Lizzie. I don't want to lose contact with you again. Ever. Is that all right, with you?'

'It is, Alfred. Now off you go before his lordship starts wondering where his pyjamas are!'

★ ★ ★

Christmas Morning brought family members and the visiting viscount to the breakfast table at varying times. Rupert strolled downstairs at around 8.30. He'd ensured the gifts he'd brought — beautifully wrapped by his valet — were easily obtainable but he rather thought the exchanging of gifts would take place that afternoon. Steadman had promised to check the family's routine with Jeffers.

'Happy Christmas,' Rupert said as he entered the dining-room.

Henry Lansdown rose from his seat and repeated the greeting.

'Please don't let me interrupt your breakfast, Henry.' Rupert headed for the buffet sideboard which was loaded with lidded dishes containing scrambled eggs, smoked bacon and sausages, kippers and kedgeree, according to the butler in attendance.

Mr Jeffers had plugged in the electric toaster, apparently a recent purchase by Mrs Lansdown. He felt, as he confided in Rupert, like a small boy with a new toy.

He took his plate to the table and looked questioningly at Henry, who was still the only other person there.

'May I sit opposite you, old chap?'

'By all means, Rupert. Did you sleep well?'

'Very well indeed. It must've been the country air. Nothing to do with the wine I put away last night, of course.'

'You single chaps have all the fun!' But Henry looked away at once, seeming to find the contents of his coffee cup extraordinarily interesting.

Rupert reckoned the eldest son had realised his faux pas and felt embarrassed. But Rupert didn't feel in the least upset. However, he couldn't help wondering whether this was what every day socialising was going to be like from now on.

He had made, he firmly believed, the correct decision, as a true gentleman should. But he found being regarded as a cad, not only irritating but hurtful, and he yearned to confide in someone.

He leaned forward.

'This information is for your ears only, Henry. I truly would appreciate your keeping it under your hat.'

Henry cleared his throat and glanced towards the butler, who was about to bring Rupert's tea to the table.

Rupert shook his head.

'A genuine chap. I asked Steadman. All I want is for at least one of your family to know that I'm not the scoundrel everyone thinks I am.'

'Gosh.' Henry speared a piece of sausage and waved his fork. 'This is to do with your broken engagement, I take it. I hadn't actually heard about it until we arrived yesterday. London gossip isn't on my agenda.'

Rupert laughed.

'Jolly good show. But you'll understand my feelings, no doubt?'

'Absolutely. If you're being accused of doing something you didn't do, no wonder you feel aggrieved.'

'Your tea, my lord.' Mr Jeffers placed a bone china cup beside Rupert's plate.

'Thanks, Jeffers.' Rupert sniffed the air. 'Can I smell burning?'

'Oh, good grief!' The butler moved swiftly to the table and rescued Rupert's slightly charred toast from the machine.

'I like mine well done,' Rupert called.

'You were saying?' Henry looked at the viscount. 'My parents will be down any minute, I expect.'

'Right.' Rupert buttered a slice of toast. 'To put it in a nutshell, my former fiancée accepted an invitation to dine with another man whilst I was out of town. When I found out from someone in my circle, who'd actually spotted them together, well, I was none too pleased.'

'I can imagine,' Henry said.

'But when I tackled Velma, my then fiancée, she threw herself on my mercy.'

Henry listened while Rupert described how he'd opted to take the blame, so that Velma's reputation might remain intact. He'd caused an uproar amongst London society and for that reason, his father had engineered the invitation to join the Lansdown family's house party.

'I can't tell you how sorry I am,' Henry said, as his parents entered the room. 'Let's try and have a chat later. I hate the thought of you being under a cloud — it's really not cricket, old chap.'

* * *

As soon as Lizzie Potter heard about the daughter of the house's predicament, she'd sent her an arnica preparation via Mr Jeffers.

Eleanor awoke on Christmas morning, delighted to discover her swollen ankle was not quite as troublesome as it had been the day before.

She agreed to her mother's suggestion of breakfast in bed, hoping further rest would allow her to enjoy more time with her twin nephews, whose company she enjoyed.

When her bedroom curtains were

opened, she was dismayed to see a flake or two of snow drifting from a leaden sky.

A parlour maid, who had carried Eleanor's tray upstairs, brought the tempting food over to the bed.

'Are you comfortable, Miss Eleanor?' she asked.

'I'm in no pain, Lucy, but worried about the weather. It looks very much as if we shall have snow and the Hunt's arranged for tomorrow. What a nuisance.'

'The children will be pleased, miss.'

Eleanor sipped her tea.

'Of course. I shall no doubt miss all the fun if we do have a heavy snowfall. And as for my poor horse . . . Stella will have no-one to ride her if the Hunt goes ahead.'

'Pardon me saying so, miss, but I heard Mr Steadman talk about the viscount's horsemanship. Could he maybe help?'

The invalid closed her eyes briefly. Lucy was trying to cheer her up, but

Stella's mistress had no desire to feel obligated to the disgraced viscount.

'Thank you, Lucy,' she said. 'I expect something can be sorted out. I'd better let you go now.'

After finishing her breakfast, Eleanor rang for help with getting washed and dressed. She often looked after her own needs, not approving of servants having to carry out such tasks for her, but today she felt at a disadvantage, and the sooner she could get downstairs and find out what everyone was up to, the better she would feel.

Peace on Earth?

Whilst being carried downstairs, Eleanor was disconcerted to see Lord Rupert crossing the hallway, noticing her descent and promptly looking very odd indeed. He almost seemed distraught. What, she wondered, could that be about?

The viscount hastened to open the door to the drawing-room, wishing her the compliments of the season, to which she responded quickly, even finding a smile for him.

It was, after all, a special day. Peace on earth and goodwill to all, she told herself as she was carried to a small couch where she could sit with her feet up.

Having been instructed to call his lordship by his name, she lost no time in quizzing him as he hovered by the nearest window.

'Rupert, are you intending to hunt tomorrow, if the snow doesn't spoil proceedings? I know the children will love having snowball fights but Boxing Day won't be the same without the Meet.'

'I'm afraid the Almighty won't care a fig about we mere mortals and our plans,' her father chipped in from his armchair.

'Anyway, my dear, you can't possibly ride. It's far too soon after your mishap.'

His daughter narrowed her eyes.

'Twenty-four hours can make a huge difference, Pa.'

'How did you churchgoers get on?' Henry rode to the rescue, before either parent could utter a word. 'Millie and I plan on taking the twins to this morning's service, if we can prise them away from their whips and tops and tin trumpets. They woke us at six, desperate to open their stockings!'

His sister shot him a grateful glance. Several people started talking and she called to her nephews to show her the exciting toys they'd found in their stockings earlier.

A large pile of parcels was heaped beneath the tree and all of a sudden, she found herself feeling ashamed that she had nothing to give Rupert.

Had her mother done something about this? Most hostesses kept a drawer containing suitable and safe gifts to wrap up in this kind of situation, but her mother had been distracted and pulled in different directions over the last couple of days.

Coffee was being served and the sweet spicy aroma of hot mince pies wafted her way, tempting her, despite her recent breakfast.

The children had been whisked off to be made ready for church and out of the corner of her eye, she noticed Rupert, standing beside his hostess, but looking her way. Her mother, she noticed, was pouring coffee for him.

'Mrs . . . I mean, Sophie, you are kindness itself.'

She saw her mother whisper in his ear then, to her dismay, Rupert walked over and seated himself on the vacant chair close by.

'I hope you don't mind my joining you, Eleanor. Dare I hope your ankle is not troubling you so much today?'

She made the mistake of locking gazes with him. Prejudice. Speculation. Disapproval. Even sanity. All of these vanished as long as she drowned in those forget-me-not eyes. Her mince pie forgotten, she struggled for a response, terrified he might guess her feelings.

But courtesy demanded she answer him, especially with her mother not far away and probably eavesdropping.

'Thank you for enquiring. Please don't tell our doctor, but I used a preparation supplied by our cook and I really believe it's helping. Also, my aunt kindly bandaged my ankle up again. She was a nurse during the Great War.'

His eyes were twinkling. Her cheeks were feeling warmer by the second.

'I heard a few of your aunt's reminiscences at dinner last night,' Rupert said. 'Hester is a redoubtable soul. There's quite an age gap between her and your mother, I imagine?'

'Yes, Aunt Hester is well into her sixties.' She lowered her voice. 'As for my mother, let's say she's somewhere between twenty-one and fifty.'

'A lady's prerogative,' Rupert agreed, his eyes sparkling with mirth.

He placed his cup on the coffee table between them.

'Eleanor, your father mentioned finding me a mount when we chatted before dinner last night. If it's any help to you, I will happily ride Stella to tomorrow's Meet.'

He ended in a hurry and she got the impression he was holding his breath. Would she trust him? Put her faith in him to take good care of her adored, spirited mare? Suddenly she felt she could.

He might be a full-blooded bounder, but to be fair, she still didn't know the true facts of the society scandal that caused him to bury himself in a country manor with people, none of whom boasted one title amongst them.

But he seemed totally at ease now. He answered to Rupert or my lord, or Lord Colford, and even to Your Worship when one of the staff became confused while serving at table for the first time. He'd caught her eye, causing both of them to seek a handkerchief and bury their faces without delay.

Her new confidant, Alfred, had hinted of his lordship's gentlemanly conduct, his integrity and some other virtue temporarily escaping her because, to her dismay, she felt as though she was floating on a fluffy pink cloud.

Alfred had spoken disparagingly of the Honourable Velma St Clair, saying the viscount was well rid of her.

She needed to respond to the viscount's offer. He would wonder what was wrong with her. The elusive tribute popped into her head. Protective.

That's what Alfred Steadman had said. Protective of a lady's virtue and well-being. Protective of his staff, too. What more could she ask for?

'If you're happy to ride my horse, Rupert, I'm happy for you to do so. But I shall be madly jealous.' She kept her gaze on her uneaten mince pie.

He reached across and picked up the plate, breaking the luscious goody into two.

'Shall we go halves?'

Wordlessly she picked up her half. When they'd each finished, he leaned across and gently dabbed her lower lip with a napkin. Startled, she touched her fingers to her lips.

'The merest, tiniest of crumbs. Please pardon my impertinence, and thank you for giving me your permission to ride Stella.' He hesitated.

'You're trusting me with something that's very precious to you. Rest assured I shall do everything in my power to take care of her.'

Later, when rerunning this scene in

her head while resting in her room before Christmas dinner, Miss Eleanor Lansdown realised that was the moment when she fell in love with Lord Rupert Colford.

★ ★ ★

Rupert strode towards his bedroom window and back again towards the door. He set off once more, to stand, arms folded, gazing at the rolling downs of Wiltshire. The snow might have fizzled out like a damp squib but that shouldn't apply to his reasoning powers.

His recent romantic palaver was a life lesson. Those first heady days with Velma catapulted him from jolly bachelor about town to devoted fiancé, ridiculously fast. He'd been gullible. His friends assured him debutantes' mothers in London and the shires considered him to be a good catch for their daughters. He found this embarrassing, but doubtless true, if all you cared about was bloodlines and a family pile.

Velma's parents had decided he would make a suitable match for their glamorous daughter. His future in-laws hadn't bargained on their daughter becoming besotted with an older man she met at a dinner party hosted by the Prince of Wales.

Rupert was out of town on business and it was at the next meeting between Velma and the gentleman in question that a friend of Rupert's caught sight of them and felt it his duty to report it to the viscount.

Thanks to his immediate decision to end the engagement and shoulder the blame, he was currently a social outcast. And Velma's flighty behaviour was such that it was only a matter of time before another scandal hit the society column headlines.

Maybe when it did, his perceived boorishness would be understood by those who'd thought ill of him, and more importantly, forgotten.

He'd survive. He didn't begrudge the alibi provided in order to spare the lady's blushes. What they had shared wasn't true love. He knew that now. What he did very much begrudge was how Eleanor found it so difficult to deal with him.

She was six years younger than he was, and a somewhat reluctant debutante in love with life, with her horse and her twin nephews. She intrigued him and he longed to get to know her better, even though her chilliness indicated she viewed him as a piece of pond life.

Yet when he and Steadman came upon her and offered their assistance, he and Eleanor had looked at each other and he could have sworn there was some sort of lightning moment, though he'd previously believed that kind of thing only happened in the romantic novels his sister and mother read.

Hearing a discreet tap at the door, he swung round.

'Enter.'

His valet appeared.

'Pardon me, my lord, but I wanted to bring your evening wear upstairs, out of the way.'

'All go down there, I imagine, Steadman?'

'Yes, sir. But in a good way.'

'Tell me, Alfred. Have you ever been in love?

'That's a strange question,' Alfred replied.

'I know, but I've never posed it to anyone before and I have concerns, you see, Alfred.'

Steadman didn't reply, but a little smile played around his lips as he moved to the wardrobe and hung the impeccably pressed shirt and evening suit inside.

'Here's the thing! I'm experiencing a feeling I never, ever, felt with you-know-who. It's nothing like that dippy, dizzy whirligig of the Velma days. It's more of a coming home feeling. Of feeling warm and fuzzy and happy. I'm

86

excited, but scared witless that the object of my affections sees me as an upper-class twit.'

'I see.'

'The young lady in question knows only the facts I saw fit to trot out to her father. Consequently, she views me with as much favour as she'd give a week-old fillet of sole.'

'Surely not, my lord?'

'Oh, but I think so.' Rupert managed an apologetic smile. 'I have struck up a rapport with Henry and he seems a decent cove. But he doesn't know me as well as you do. Most of my friends and unquestionably my parents, view me as a dead loss just now, and if I even hinted how I'd fallen for another girl, I'd be laughed out of town, don't you think?'

'With respect, my lord, none of the folk you mention are in the vicinity.'

'Something to be thankful for, I suppose.' Rupert began pacing back and forth again.

'Christmas can be an emotional time,

sir. It's when families gather, so maybe you miss your own loved ones more than you realise.'

Rupert stopped in his tracks.

'Right. So, you think I should ignore these peculiar feelings and put them down to the time of year?'

'If it's of any help and if the object of your lordship's affections is the young lady whom I assume it must be, I think you should credit her with the wit to recognise your true character — even if it takes a while longer than you'd wish.'

'Right. That is sensible advice, Steadman, much as I'd expect from an upright fellow like you.' He consulted his watch. 'I'd better get a shift on. Having not made it last night, I'd better not miss the service this morning.'

'I was about to remind you, my lord.' Steadman disappeared into the adjoining dressing-room and emerged carrying Rupert's overcoat, trilby, muffler and gloves.

'So, Steadman, did you attend Midnight Mass as you thought you might? I forgot to enquire before. I decided to keep the elderly aunt company. She's formidable but quite a character — doesn't seem the least bit bothered by my recent predicament. In fact, she confessed to having been involved in one or two scandals herself!'

The valet helped the viscount into his coat.

'I attended church, my lord. It was a very satisfactory experience. And I've got to know one or two of the staff a little better.'

'Good show. They certainly know how to produce decent food. More than decent, in fact.' He wound his scarf around his neck.

Steadman handed Rupert his gloves.

'It is possible the elderly lady has found a kindred spirit in you, my lord.'

'Well, it's good to know at least one female doesn't consider me a scally-wag!' Rupert plonked the trilby on his head.

'I think Miss Eleanor's mother would hardly label you as such, sir.'

'You don't miss much, do you, old chap?' Rupert headed for the door.

Left alone to tidy the room, Alfred mused how Christmas was indeed the time for family to come together. How ironic it was, to be spending the festive season in the same house as Lizzie Potter — his Lizzie, as he still thought of her — as well as her daughter.

But he had no right to regard either of them as family and, realising this, he felt as though a black cloud enveloped him.

The Food of Love

Lizzie Potter gazed around at the area she often likened to a stage. She, of course, took the leading role, supported by Violet and Emmie. Today, Alfred Steadman and the footman would assist Mr Jeffers in the dining-room. Counting everyone staying in the house, plus three dear friends of her employers, there would be 13 sitting down to the four o'clock dinner.

She'd coped before and she knew she'd cope now, even though she'd spent a chunk of the night time hours tossing and turning before finally falling asleep. Had Alfred been affected in the same way, she wondered. Probably she'd never know, but she didn't have time to daydream. Not when she had oysters to grill without turning the delicate shellfish to chewy rubber.

Mock turtle soup simmered in a big pan on the hob. The seafood platter rested on a marble slab in the pantry, awaiting her attentions. Beef Wellington, crisp pastry crust concealing succulent meat, rested in the warming oven, while in the main oven, a stuffed goose was roasting to perfection. Soon its golden-brown skin would crackle and yield to the carving knife's sharp blade.

Lizzie had prepared Brussels sprouts with chestnuts, braised red cabbage and apple, plus the usual root vegetables.

A plum pudding fit to grace King George's table still steamed gently, while Emmie's Buche de Noel, its likeness to a log and its chocolate flavour certain to delight the children, waited in the wings along with her marzipan fruits, miniature meringues and brandy truffles.

A glass bowl of fruit salad was not forgotten either.

The pungent scent of sizzling garlic butter filled the kitchen as Emmie hovered, two serving dishes at the ready. Lizzie turned around immediately the juicy oysters began curling at their edges.

'Here we go, Emmie!' She removed the huge grill pan from the heat. 'First batch coming up.'

So began the production line. Pans removed. Pans added. Staff instructed. Vegetables drained. Gravy stirred and until not one lump dared spoil its rich smoothness. Faces were flushed with heat but everything went smoothly, much to the relief of Lizzie.

'I think that Mr Steadman's ever so nice,' Emmie said after she and her mother watched the men set off with the goose and all its trimmings. 'Funny how he really did turn out old enough to be my father.'

'Has he been talking to you?' Lizzie felt her heart beat faster. She should have thought of this possibility.

'Only to thank me for dishing up his breakfast.'

'Serving his breakfast, Emmie. And

93

don't mutter under your breath like that. I'm only trying to help you sound less like a country bumpkin.'

'Whatever for?'

Her daughter's indignant expression made Lizzie laugh.

'It's important to speak well nowadays, silly. Times are changing and you won't always want to work as a kitchen maid, will you?'

Emmie gasped. She lifted a lid.

'They've forgotten to take in the devils on horseback. See?'

'Oh, my word — and thirteen at table today! Let's hope nothing else goes wrong. Take them through to Mr Jeffers, or — or, Mr Steadman, whoever's closest.'

'Can't Violet go?'

Lizzie placed the serving dish on a tray.

'Move. Say nothing and pray the old lady hasn't noticed her favourites are missing. Though, given half a chance, she'd wolf the lot, according to Mr Jeffers.'

94

Emmie nodded and did as her mother asked.

Lizzie sank down on the chair beside the range. Her thoughts kept returning to Alfred Steadman. Seeing him again stirred old memories, releasing emotions kept hidden for years. But this was no time for restless thoughts.

Lizzie saw Violet give her a curious look as the girl carried yet another load of dirty plates to the sink.

'Cheer up, Violet. We'll have extra pairs of hands for the Boxing Day party.'

'I don't know how you cope with it all, Cook, and that's a fact. My hands get so red and sore.'

'Think about the lovely meal we'll be eating later, soon as everything's sorted in the dining-room. Mr Lansdown always comes and pours us each a glass of wine.'

'Even me?'

'Even you. Miss Eleanor likes to help wait on us but she won't be doing that today. Not with that gammy ankle, she won't.'

Violet summoned up a smile.

'I'm glad I works here, Mrs P. A friend of mine's a skivvy in a place where there's a right old dragon of a cook.'

'I shan't comment, Vi. Always remember the post goes both ways. You're a good worker and you and Emmie get on. Watch and learn and who knows where it might lead.'

Rupert decided, if he closed his eyes, he'd still know it was Christmas Day. That combination of Scots pine, candles burning, roasted meats and cinnamon and oranges, was unmistakeable. He was enjoying his day far more than he imagined he would, after accepting Edward Lansdown's invitation.

By some magical means, each of the twins had discovered a shiny silver sixpence in their small portion of pudding.

Rupert suspected the family cook

and Mr Jeffers of master-minding this trick and he also approved the idea of the boys joining the grown-ups in the dining-room for the big meal. His relations mostly hid their young off-spring in the nursery on such occasions.

He'd eaten numerous dinners at his family home, and at that of his former fiancée and, to his surprise, found the company here jollier. He'd laughed to hear of a prank George confided to him, but on realising what his host was saying, turned his attention to it.

'I shall of course do my usual stint for the staff meal,' Mr Lansdown said.

Rupert missed hearing what the vicar had asked Edward Lansdown, but the reply was perfectly audible and provided Rupert with food for thought.

'I help to serve them at table. Pour them all a glass of wine and thank them for their hard work. Usually, my daughter helps pass the food around and so forth, but unfortunately that's impossible this time.'

Those within hearing made sympathetic noises. Rupert wondered if the vicar was debating whether to offer assistance or whether to stay put, in case he missed another round of food.

He chided himself over such an uncharitable sentiment when he was the outsider. He definitely shouldn't harbour such feelings towards a man of the cloth and suddenly he thought what fun it might be to take Eleanor's place.

Ignoring the possibility of any ulterior motive, he took a deep breath.

'Excuse me, Edward, but I wonder whether I might help you? It's the least I can do when you're welcoming me into your home and entertaining me so royally. I couldn't have wished for a more mouthwatering dinner, enjoyed in such congenial company.'

Rupert thought Edward looked uncertain, though his wife was beaming and even the vicar was nodding approval.

'Pa? I think you should accept Rupert's kind offer,' Eleanor said.

Her father smiled at Rupert.

'There's really no need, my lord. It's an honour to have you staying with us.'

'Please do call me Rupert. I have no wish to stand on ceremony, particularly on a day like today.'

'Oh, do say yes, Pa! If Rupert helps you, I won't feel so guilty about letting everyone down,' Eleanor said.

'My daughter thinks she can wind me around her little finger, Rupert. I wouldn't dream of imposing on you.'

'Well, I meant what I said and apart from anything else, my valet will be highly entertained to have me waiting on him.' Rupert beamed. 'Quite right, too!'

His host laughed.

'Ah, well, who am I to spoil the fun? Everyone sits down at seven-thirty. There'll be a cold spread left for us on the sideboard in here and we won't be gone too long.'

Rupert noticed the vicar's eyes gleam. No doubt the old boy was in seventh heaven! He longed to share his own joke with Eleanor.

'I can't imagine being able to face even a biscuit after that amazing meal. When you're ready to go, please let me know. I shan't be far away.'

Silently he reflected how much he'd dreaded joining the party and how he planned to plead a headache and retire to his bedroom and read 'The Great Gatsby', a copy of which he'd brought with him just in case.

But despite her initial frostiness, even Eleanor appeared more at ease in his company now. Even if she'd decided to bury the hatchet only for the next couple of days, it was far more preferable than getting the cold shoulder.

He looked across at her again and she averted her eyes, but to his delight, swiftly sneaked another peep at him. He wondered if she'd been checking to see if he was still gazing in her direction.

The twins had been allowed to get down from table and had promptly raced towards the sitting-room with their father in hot pursuit. Rupert grinned as he remembered behaving in exactly the same way at their age.

What the devil had Steadman chosen for the twins? He should have asked him but with so much on his mind over the Velma fiasco, gifts for strangers had been the last thing on his mind. And now this family, in a very short space of time, were no longer strangers.

While chatting with George, the younger son had confessed to having a crush on the cook's daughter and wasn't sure whether anyone had said anything or not but his father had advised him not to pester the girl.

This had led to a fascinating discussion about the British class system with Rupert and George agreeing that Starminster Manor's staff seemed happy with their lot, but one day, life for everyone would become very different, due to so much progress in industry and technology.

Mr and Mrs Lansdown led the way from the dining-room, but everyone, in their eagerness, had obviously forgotten poor Eleanor. Rupert was about to approach her and offer his assistance when his valet, standing with Mr Jeffers while they waited to clear the table, practically leapt to help her.

'You beat me to it, Steadman,' Rupert said and grinned good-naturedly. 'Can you manage, old chap?'

'He's not that old, Rupert!' Eleanor retorted. 'Thank you so much, Alfred. I purposely didn't eat too much plum pudding.'

'If I may say so, Miss Eleanor, you are as light as the proverbial feather.'

Rupert, watching Alfred scoop up the invalid with no trouble at all, was, for once, speechless.

★ ★ ★

In the drawing-room there was already a sea of paper and string upon the carpet beneath the fir tree, its branches adorned with silver and gold baubles.

Most of the gifts were for the two little boys but everyone received a miniature prayer book from the crotchety clergyman, as Rupert had disrespectfully nicknamed him, although for George's and Eleanor's ears only.

But Rupert felt extraordinarily touched by the gesture and was pleased he'd included the vicar and his wife on the gift list.

Rupert's bottles of port wine for the gentlemen plus splendid gift-wrapped boxes of chocolates for the ladies were received with much delight.

Alfred Steadman, he reflected, was an absolute gem and he'd be lost without him. He was a walking diary, a chef, a chess opponent, chauffeur, etiquette expert and confidant all rolled into one.

He didn't appear to have a special lady in his life, but maybe he was waiting for the right one to come along. He had certainly made a hit with the daughter of the house, that was for sure.

'My goodness,' Rupert exclaimed as he unwrapped a paisley-patterned silk cravat. 'Thank you so much, Sophie. I shall wear this with pride.' He was also touched when he opened a hand-drawn greetings card from the twins. Their joint effort was a drawing of a horse looking up at a rather wobbly star in the sky above.

His gifts to them of model aeroplanes were a great success and when the boys, prompted by their mother, offered shy thanks, Rupert said he'd pass these on to Mr Steadman whom he was sure had asked Santa Claus for advice in choosing the toys.

Electric lamps were helping the candlelight as day dissolved into dusk. Just after 7.30, Mr Jeffers informed his master that the staff were assembled. On their way to the kitchen, Rupert learned a little about the way the household ran.

'In their own sitting-room they take turns to make up the fire. When they're not on duty, they can sit there, rather than hang around the kitchen or their bedrooms.'

'If I may say so, you have a very enlightened view when it comes to dealings with servants. I find it most refreshing.'

'My wife and I pride ourselves on maintaining a happy staff. We're fortunate in that most of them have been with us a while though I get the feeling Emmie might be ready to spread her wings soon. Her mother has taught her well and the daughter has a talent for creating spectacular cakes and desserts.'

'So I've noticed.' Rupert could hear the buzz of anticipation from inside the kitchen as he followed his host through the door.

'Happy Christmas, sir!' The chorus of voices sang out. Seeing Rupert, one or two people called out a greeting to him and, prompted everyone else to chime in.

Rupert was delighted to note that a dark green chenille cloth covered the long table in the centre of the room. Sprigs of scarlet-berried holly and white-painted fire cones were dotted about, with a festive cracker beside each place.

Jeffers had already uncorked two bottles of wine and delegated the task of pouring to Rupert while Emmie and Violet brought dishes of vegetables to the table and Edward Lansdown doled out slices of roast turkey, already expertly sliced by Cook.

There was a moment of silence then Rupert was surprised to hear his valet say Grace. Everyone murmured 'Amen' then glasses were raised in a toast to the master. Mr Lansdown responded by thanking them all for their hard work and by complimenting Cook and her team for a magnificent Christmas dinner. Rupert chimed in.

'Hear, hear!'

'I'm glad you were pleased, sir.' Lizzie, still standing, bobbed smoothly. 'Thank you too, my lord. I can take the weight off my feet now.' She raised her glass to the two gentlemen.

Jeffers sprang to his feet and proposed a toast.

'To Mr Lansdown and his good lady. The finest employers in the country.'

Everyone echoed the sentiment. Rupert glanced at his valet. Mrs Potter had taken the seat next to Alfred and, as the viscount noticed the cook's bright curls, released from their usual cap, he intercepted a look passing between the two. What was that about?

He'd never seen fit to question his manservant about his personal life though he knew much about his background and how he'd fought for his country. But he'd never have put the man down as a fast worker with the ladies.

After he'd topped up glasses, joked with Tommy from the stables and made Violet and Emmie blush by admiring their best Sunday frocks, Rupert noticed his host making his way to the door. With one last glance at Lizzie Potter and Alfred, who seemed only to have eyes for one another, he made his way out too.

Sporting Chance

On Boxing Day morning, Rupert rang for his valet to help him dress in his riding habit.

'How's the weather looking, d'you reckon, Steadman? I'm grateful you made the fire up last night.'

'It's still gloomy out there, sir. Some windowpanes are iced inside, I notice.'

'Oh dear. Let's hope the snow holds off.'

'The fox will hope for a good downfall, no doubt, my lord?'

'Hmm. I'm partly on the side of Reynard, as you know. There must be something about my personality preventing me from offending people who feel strongly that blood sports are important.'

'I believe you enjoy the tradition and the convivial atmosphere, sir.'

'Indeed I do, Steadman. Just as I

hope you enjoyed last night's festive dinner with the new friends you've made.' He noticed Alfred's eyes gleam.

'It was splendid, sir. And may I say how much everyone appreciated your attendance? You were rated a more than adequate substitute for Miss Eleanor.'

'Praise indeed. Now, I must go and see if I'm still allowed to ride her horse.'

'I can tell you the young lady already rang to request a lift downstairs, my lord.'

'Did she, indeed? I'd better show my face then.' Rupert loped downstairs and entered the dining-room, to find Eleanor and her father already at table, eating porridge.

'Good morning! You're up and about early, my boy. Do join us.' Edward Lansdown beamed at his guest.

Rupert greeted Eleanor just as George entered the room.

'Good heavens, this must be a miracle. My younger son up and about by nine!'

'Very droll, Pa.' George sauntered

over to the sideboard. 'Coffee and toast for me, please, Jeffers. He helped himself to kedgeree and sat down opposite his sister.

'What can I get you, my lord?' Jeffers had noticed Rupert standing to one side.

'Oh, um, eggs and bacon, I think, Jeffers. With toast and coffee, too, please.'

He took the seat next to George.

'Sorry, everyone, I was just thinking what a good day it was yesterday.'

Eleanor looked at him with what he considered to be suspicion.

'Really? It was only our usual sort of Christmas Day.'

Rupert stared back at her.

'After what I've endured the last week or so, being down here with all of you making me feel so welcome, is heaven.'

He noticed no-one met his eyes. He waited for Eleanor or even George to protest that surely his uncomfortable days after breaking off his engagement were his own fault. But nobody said a word. He was on the verge of breaking his vow to keep Velma's behaviour a secret when his host broke the silence.

'It's a pleasure to have you with us, Rupert. And if ever you need to find a bolthole again, you know you'll be most welcome.'

'Thank you, Edward. That is most kind and much appreciated, but I hope never to find myself in such a tricky situation again.'

Rupert got the feeling everyone was trying to think of something to fill the awkward silence. Mr Jeffers took away Eleanor's porridge bowl and came back with two boiled eggs and a plate of toast.

'May I ask how your ankle's feeling today, Eleanor?' her father asked.

'It's much better, thank you, Pa. I'm hoping another three or four days will see me back in the saddle. Not to mention walking up and downstairs on my own.'

'I shall do my absolute best to remain

in my saddle today,' Rupert said.

Mr Lansdown chuckled.

'Stella's a docile enough horse if you know what you're doing, which I imagine you do, young man. And we have an excellent Master so we should have a good day as long as snow only threatens, rather than falls.'

'It would be disappointing if snow stopped play,' Rupert said.

'I'm really annoyed I can't take part. I wonder if I could join the hunt followers,' Eleanor said.

Rupert inclined his head. She'd caught him with his mouth full of toast, but his host came to the rescue.

'Over my dead body, young lady! Didn't the doctor advise you to rest your foot until he comes back to examine it again?'

'But, Pa, the swelling has almost vanished and I fear my brain will explode if I'm forced to read Aunt Hester even one more paragraph of 'Wuthering Heights'. And as for those interminable card games with those

silly little red and black symbols . . . '
She finished with a huff.

Rupert fixed his gaze on his willow-patterned plate though found difficulty in restraining a smile.

'That's all very well, daughter, but I still recommend you stay put this morning. Please let that be an end to the matter.'

Other family members were coming in for breakfast as Rupert wondered who would ultimately win the argument. Something about the pretty debutante's tilted chin hinted at a Boudica dressed for battle beneath that attractive exterior. He was getting to like this young woman more and more.

★   ★   ★

Accompanied on horseback by his host and Eleanor's brother Henry, Rupert felt energised by the cold snapping air and the prospect of a good gallop.

The hunt members gathered outside

a nearby hostelry, taking a cup of mulled wine to warm the cockles while Mr Lansdown took the opportunity to introduce his guest to his friends, all of whom were attending the party at the manor house later.

Two or three of them looked bemused on hearing his full title but Rupert felt he'd got off lightly. Things could be rather different that evening, but he'd meet that possibility when it came to it.

It was while crossing a field, hounds baying, horses galloping at full tilt, his breath like white smoke, merging with Stella's, he noticed the unmistakeable, tall bowler-hatted figure of his valet, standing beyond the wall separating field from highway.

Nor was Alfred Steadman alone. Beside him stood a young woman wearing a camel hair overcoat, her hair concealed by a crimson felt cloche hat. But without doubt it was Eleanor gripping the top bar of the gate with both gloved hands.

Rupert's groan of longing melted into the cacophony of men shouting and hounds baying. He pretended not to notice her, but knew Steadman must have driven the Bentley and would only have done so because she'd coaxed him, knowing he was putty in her hands. The impudence of her!

Yet he hoped her father hadn't spotted her, even though she was no longer a child. Her impetuous nature both astonished and attracted Rupert, too accustomed to simpering heiresses and predatory young women who were out for a good time while keeping their marriage options open.

* * *

'With the greatest of respect, my lord, under the circumstances I didn't consider the request unreasonable.' Steadman helped his employer off with his jacket.

'Is that so? Did she not tell you her father expressly forbade her to follow on foot? Understandably he didn't wish her to aggravate the state of her ankle.

'You were with me when we went to her aid on Christmas Eve. You're clearly more in favour than I am, even though she entrusted me with her beloved horse today.

'Didn't you suspect she was taking advantage of the soft spot you have for her, by asking you to steal my car and drive her to watch the hunt?'

Rupert watched a slow blush suffuse his valet's cheeks. He'd trust his man with his life. He'd lend him the Bentley without a second thought. But he was cross with him for conspiring with Eleanor. Jealous, even.

'Mr Steadman, that young woman shouldn't have tried walking any greater distance than from the dining-room to the sitting-room. Who knows if between the pair of you, you haven't put her recovery back by several days? Even damaged her ankle permanently.'

'I can assure you the young lady did not have occasion to bear her weight, negligible as it is, while under my care, sir.'

Rupert's eyebrows rocketed.

'Did someone provide a bath chair? Stop trying to pull the wool over my eyes!'

'I can assure you that I carried Miss Eleanor from the sitting-room to the rear door of the domestic quarters, where she rested in a chair provided by, erm, one of the staff.'

'That would be the magnificent Mrs Potter, I presume. Another of your conquests.'

He saw the gleam in the older man's eyes and suspected his valet was enjoying the sparring as much as he was.

'Miss Eleanor and I had already, erm, hatched a plan.' Steadman held out a freshly ironed shirt. 'While I moved the Bentley closer to the back door, two of the lads carried her out and helped her into the back seat, so she could sit with both her — well, without having to keep her feet on the floor.'

'She would of course know precisely where to find an excellent view of the hunt. No doubt you were able to carry her the short distance from the car to the grass verge where she could lean on the gate.'

Steadman nodded.

But Rupert could no longer keep up his onslaught. Peals of laughter rang out, while he watched his valet's face contort as he tried to maintain composure.

'Don't worry, Alfred. I shan't sneak on the pair of you. I don't think for one minute our host noticed, and if he did, he's keeping it under his hat.'

'Thank you, sir. I apologise if my behaviour seemed inappropriate.'

'Truth is, old chap, Miss Eleanor could charm a tasty bone from a grumpy bulldog! She shouldn't have involved you, but I understand it must have been difficult for you to refuse, given we're guests here.'

Famished by frosty air and exercise, Rupert descended, to the dining-room.

The rest of the family, apart from Eleanor and her father, had already eaten.

'Come and sit down, dear boy,' Edward Lansdown said. 'I was just telling my daughter what an excellent morning we had. Top marks for acquitting yourself so well.'

'I should also say, one of the maids told me they enjoyed meeting you last night. I gather you gained a round of applause,' Eleanor said.

'You're very kind, both of you. It was good to see your staff enjoying themselves. As for today, all credit should go to a certain lady. She's really rather wonderful. Beautiful, too. Definitely a spirited filly who needs firm handling, but with such very satisfactory results.'

The words were addressed to Edward Lansdown, but the viscount's gaze held Eleanor's. He felt tremendous satisfaction seeing her cheeks turn a fetching shade of pink before she switched her attention to her bread and butter.

Unwelcome Visitor

Eleanor faced a dilemma. She daren't risk dancing even one step when the party moved into the big reception room where musicians held court. She didn't want to seem discourteous, but could she really face joining Aunt Hester and her cronies on the sidelines?

She stared at her reflection in the dressing table mirror. There would be young women at the party whom she knew and, in some cases, whose company she enjoyed. There could even be a young man or two who'd seek her out and keep her champagne glass filled.

The most disturbing thing of all was how much her attitude had changed towards the visiting viscount. This began even before her little jaunt with his valet provided the perfect opportunity to press Alfred into disclosing events leading to the end of his master's betrothal.

Her problem lay in allowing her former chilliness towards Rupert to melt away. He'd surely wonder at this, and might well suspect she'd coaxed confidential information from his faithful servant. She hated the thought of Alfred coming under fire for indiscretion.

The valet had made it clear this was highly confidential information and he was only telling her because it so grieved him to see her viewing the viscount as some sort of bounder with no respect of a lady's feelings.

Yet to maintain her *froideur* — to quote one of Aunt Hester's favourite expressions — and stay distanced from a man who'd smashed through her original perceptions simply by being himself — didn't appeal.

Any gentleman prepared to place his reputation on the line to protect his treacherous former betrothed must possess a steadfastness Eleanor found lacking in most of the men her mother considered husband material.

But the viscount was way out of Eleanor's league and her mother should accept it. Alfred had said only good things about his employer and Eleanor trusted his judgement.

Sadly, the picture painted of Velma and her scandalous behaviour was an eye-opener. She promised herself, if any of her parents' guests spotted the viscount and began spreading vile rumours, she, Eleanor, would put paid to such mischief in no uncertain manner.

This decision calmed her. As to how she would carry out this threat, given she'd be draped over the furniture like Cleopatra on her barge, was a different matter. Eleanor would need to lurk in a corner where she'd be available but not in anyone's way.

The only consolation was not being required to take to the floor with one drippy youth after the other. Most of them were more concerned with their own images than with interesting topics like horses, cars and aeroplanes.

Her mother employed a girl from the nearby village to take care of her wardrobe and help dress her hair for social engagements. Earlier, Eleanor's hair had been styled, not tortured, so catching sight of her reflection in the looking glass didn't displease her, especially as her dress, a symphony of pinks, clung and swung in all the right places.

Shoes were a problem until her mother, who took a size larger than Eleanor, produced a pair of white satin slippers. For the first time since the afternoon of Christmas Eve, she would tackle the stairs, even if hanging on to her brother George's arm.

When she heard him knock, she invited him to enter before rising to face the door. She almost sat straight down again.

'How beautiful you are, Eleanor.' The viscount walked towards her. 'Please permit me to escort you to the party.

George is entertaining your nephews with a thrilling tale of pirates, sharks and treasure, so I'm here in his place.'

'Goodness.' She swallowed hard. 'That's a side of my brother I've never seen.'

'People are not always what we think them to be.' Rupert spoke softly.

Her tummy somersaulted. She'd never been one to swoon over handsome young men, usually finding them far too shallow for her liking. But seeing this one beside her, so close, with such a tender expression on his face, she knew there was no use in fighting her feelings.

'I expect my mother would swoon if she knew you were alone with me in my room.'

'Am I in danger, Eleanor? I do hope so!' His blue eyes sparkled.

They faced each other. She should take his arm. Begin walking. Instead she placed both hands lightly upon his broad shoulders and tilted her face upwards. His mouth was close. So very

124

close. She shut her eyes, hoping he couldn't hear the thumping of her heart. This, she decided, was a young man she could trust.

'Eleanor!' Footsteps treading the landing. A man's voice calling from outside her door.

At once she turned away from Rupert. He put his arm around her waist as support.

'Come in, Henry. What is it?'

Her elder brother stood in the doorway.

'Forgive me for interrupting, sis, but I have a message for you, Rupert.'

'For me? Who is it from, Henry?'

'Your former fiancée has arrived and is, um, demanding to see you.'

Eleanor watched the viscount's face drain of colour.

'Velma's here? You mean she has gatecrashed your party? I can't apologise enough.'

'She's not exactly gate-crashing, but you'd better go down and talk to her. I'll see my sister descends in one piece.'

Henry stepped forward.

Rupert relaxed his hold on Eleanor. At once she felt bereft. So many questions remained unanswered and she could only imagine his anguish at this strange development.

He shot her a pleading look.

'I'm so sorry. I have no idea what's brought about this astonishingly rude behaviour.'

'It's best you do as Henry suggests, my lord.'

The look of desolation in Rupert's eyes when she spoke so formally to him left her yearning to reach out to him. But the story she suspected might have been beginning, seemed destined to remain untold.

On entering Sophie Lansdown's cosy sitting-room, Rupert was met by an all-too-familiar exotic scent. He closed the door behind him.

'What's this about, Velma? Have you no shame?'

'Dear Rupert, always so passionate about what's right and what's wrong.

It's wonderful to see you, but do try to keep your voice down, darling.' The Honourable Velma St Clair smiled up at him from the crimson velvet couch.

'Any numbskull would know how wrong it is to turn up here, uninvited!' Rupert was trying to keep his temper.

'Really! I'll have you know I'm here as the guest of one of George Lansdown's friends. I'm staying in the area for a night or two. You remember Charlie Bell? He's over the moon, having me on his arm.' She patted her hair.

'Good for him. He always was a chump. How on earth did you know I was here?'

'I have my spies, darling.'

'I don't understand. Where's the actor?'

'That would-be West End star was merely a passing fancy, Rupert. I mistakenly believed I'd fallen in love. We were both carried away, but such a little fling is commonplace nowadays. You must realise that. You reacted in haste, didn't you? Come on, admit it!'

Rupert shook his head.

'Definitely not.'

She pouted.

'Surely you're just a teeny bit pleased to see me? Forgive and forget and let things return to normal?' She fluttered her eyelashes.

He felt only impatience towards her.

'You are, I'm afraid, sadly mistaken,' he said. 'I have endured much embarrassment and inconvenience since your little fling, as you regard it, ended our engagement.

'Tongues will wag again tonight, Velma, and who could blame people for gossiping? For the life of me, I can't understand why you want to turn up here, when you could be dancing the night away at some house party with your royal relation and his crowd.'

'Because, silly boy, I want you and me to become engaged again. My mother was right. We're perfect for one another so don't be boring. You know I can't bear it when you're cross.'

She gazed up at him, blinking away tears that he knew didn't exist.

'I'm not cross. Merely puzzled, after all the chaos you brought into my life, as to why you have the audacity to think I'm willing to renew our engagement — a betrothal I've since realised should never have occurred.'

She sighed.

'You can't really mean that. Your pride was wounded and you're getting your own back. It's all right. I completely understand. Can you pass me a cigarette, darling?' She eyed the cedarwood box on the nearby table.

'No. You surely haven't forgotten how much I disliked you smoking? And can't you understand I have nothing more to say to you? Except that I have absolutely no intention of making you my viscountess.'

She glanced at the exquisite diamond watch on her wrist and smiled.

'We've been closeted together all alone for a while. People will wonder what's going on, my sweet. Stop being so stubborn and come and sit over here.'

'Contrary to what you might believe, Velma, I'd rather kiss one of Edward Lansdown's horses than lower myself to embrace you.'

Her eyes narrowed.

'You're unhappy. That's why you're saying such spiteful things. After supper, I insist you dance with me, so everyone can see how civilised we are. They'll all be thrilled to see us together again. Remember those gossip column headlines?' Her expression became coy. 'The golden couple! Rupert and his ravishing Velma!'

He shook his head.

'You sicken me.'

'You'll regret this, Rupert.'

He watched her shimmy off the couch and stand upright, adjusting her pink feather boa around her slender neck. He had to admit she had style — but not his kind of style.

'My only regret is that you didn't do me this favour sooner,' he said. 'You only ever wanted me for my title. Your mother was egging you on so don't even try to deny it. Why can't you admit what you know is true?'

They glared at one another and again Rupert wondered what on earth he'd ever seen in her.

'I have to say, I think this slumming you're wallowing in, staying here with the vulgar Lansdown family has made you forget your manners. That alone will make a tasty titbit for the newspapers, my sweet, don't you think? Your dear parents will be devastated. Do they have any idea where you're spending the Christmas holiday?'

'As it happens, yes — not that it's any of your business. My host is a friend of my father's.'

To Rupert's relief, a knock at the door stopped Velma from making a further nasty remark. He hated confrontation, but couldn't let her get away with her horrible comments.

'Tell whoever it is to scram!' Velma

snapped. 'I haven't finished with you yet!'

Rupert ignored her.

'Come in.' The door opened and he had never before been so pleased to see Alfred Steadman, immaculate, implacable and immensely reassuring.

The valet bowed in Velma's direction.

'Forgive the interruption, ma'am, but I am instructed to inform my lord that supper is being served.'

Rupert breathed a sigh of relief.

'May I enquire as to who sent you, Steadman?'

Alfred held his head high.

'Why, the young lady to whom you have so recently become betrothed, my lord. I believe Miss Eleanor is anxious to introduce you to her circle of friends.'

★ ★ ★

Alfred closed the back door behind him and gazed up at the stars. Inside, the kitchen buzzed with energy as staff juggled empty plates and squirrelled away leftovers, the washers-up slaved at the vast stone sink and Lizzie Potter supervised the departure of further trays of delicacies.

Once again, he pictured the expression on the Honourable Velma's face as he dropped his bombshell. Her reaction had exceeded his wildest dreams.

For months now, he had stuck to his own low opinion of the social butterfly who'd whirled into the viscount's life and made him act like a moth blinded by bright light.

This opinion he had never revealed to his employer but he was very glad when Rupert ended the engagement, despite the fallout.

Alfred wasn't prone to eavesdropping, but having approached the sitting-room door and hearing the desperation in his lordship's voice, he glanced round to make sure no-one was nearby, and pretended to retie his shoelace.

The viscount's reaction to this most unladylike of ladies persuaded Alfred to act swiftly. At once he'd tapped on the door and entered, to tell a lie, even if a well-intentioned one. His employer had looked relieved, especially as Alfred gave him the ghost of a wink without his unwelcome visitor noticing.

This declaration set several things in motion. The Honourable Velma had collapsed on to the crimson cushions, wailing in anguish — or anger that her plan hadn't been successful. His lordship had asked Alfred to fetch a glass of water but Velma promptly stopped bawling and requested something stronger.

Alfred had hurried off to fetch not only a glass of champagne, but the lady's escort, though this gentleman was none too pleased to be deprived of continuing such a sumptuous supper.

The viscount shook hands with a disgruntled Charlie Bell, thanked him for attending and informed him his partner was indisposed. While this was most unfortunate, it was best if the couple left at once.

Rupert was sure Charlie would understand how tedious it would be to disrupt their kind hosts' annual party. Alfred, meanwhile, fetched the couple's outer garments before going outside to locate Mr Bell's chauffeur, who was hanging around in the staff sitting-room with the other drivers.

Rupert saw the couple off the premises before turning to his valet.

'My bacon, as they say, has been saved. But I don't believe for one moment Miss Eleanor sent that message!'

'My lord?'

'I'm saying, Steadman, the idea is ludicrous.'

'If you say so, sir.'

'Does anyone else know about it?'

'Of course not, my lord. You have my assurance on that.'

Rupert shook his head slowly.

'But whatever will I do if news of this second engagement leaks out, Alfred? I'll be a laughing stock again and I dread to think what Miss Eleanor will say. I'd be grateful to receive the advice of the prime mover in making this announcement.'

'Well, that would be me, sir. All I can say is, you should follow the advice of your heart, my lord. As for your former fiancée, I have a feeling she would prefer to forget her unfortunate visit this evening.'

Rupert stared back at him in silence. Until a smile, as light dawning, mingled with joy, transformed his face.

'You are, as usual, right, my friend. Thank you. Now, I must rejoin the party.' He went indoors, leaving his valet to close the front door.

Why Risk Heartache?

Alfred Steadman watched his employer hurry towards the dining-room. The gathering was only 30 or so in number, but much care had been taken to provide a scrumptious buffet and the guests wore evening dress, the ladies' gorgeous silks, satins and feathers adding to the colour and glitter radiated by the room's décor and festive decorations.

He headed down the corridor towards the domestic quarters and slipped quietly through the kitchen then out to the scullery and through the rear door to stand gazing up at the moon. A minute or so later, he felt a waft of warm air as the door opened behind him. He swung around.

'You trying to catch your death?' Lizzie handed him a cup of mulled wine. Gratefully, he smiled at her and wrapped his fingers around its warmth.

'You're an angel, Lizzie Potter. As if you haven't enough to do.'

'I noticed you sneak out here. All my hard work's done for the night so I thought I'd check up on you and leave the others to it.'

He offered her the cup.

'Take a sip or two. I can't drink alone.'

'I wouldn't normally offer alcohol when you're on duty,' she said, 'but it seemed a good idea, given the circum-stances.' She shivered.

'You'll freeze out here.' He pushed open the door and took her arm, nudging her inside. 'Nobody in the scullery at the moment so we can find a quiet corner.' He pursed his lips. 'Might I ask what exactly you've heard?'

'Only that the viscount's former fiancée turned up, escorted by a gentleman. Mr Jeffers whispered it to me.'

'He'd have let them in, no doubt.'

'He told me the lady who's related to

that Austrian count, the one they call a playboy' — she wrinkled her nose in disapproval — 'arrived, looking like a film star with her blonde curls all piled up high and wearing a fur coat.'

'And smelling like Harrod's perfume department! Who else knows, Lizzie?'

'Don't worry yourself. I told Mr Jeffers he should keep it to himself unless he wanted to live on bread, and water till Twelfth Night!'

'You're a treasure, you really are. I could hug you!'

She cleared her throat and looked anywhere but at him.

'Alfred, I realise this happening must have made life even more difficult for his lordship, but I understand if you feel you shouldn't tell me anything.'

He thought how she always did have a nice way of speaking, much more refined than most women he'd worked with in the past, unless they were governesses or ladies' maids.

'Let us just say I needed my wits about me to prevent an awkward situation from worsening. We're not quite out of the woods yet though, Lizzie. Some people can be very vindictive.'

'Not you though, Alfred. Definitely not you.'

'It's good of you to say so. Especially to the man who quit your life so suddenly, when we were getting on so well together. I still can't believe how stupid and thoughtless I was back then.'

She touched his arm. Briefly.

'I told you we can't bring back the past. I took the plunge and married someone else.' She hesitated. 'My daughter means the world to me, but if things had been different . . . '

'Don't let's torture ourselves, Lizzie. It's clear you've made a good job of bringing up your Emmie. Her father must have been proud of the pair of you. And now you're widowed and I've found you again, I'd like to do my bit to help.'

'That's very kind, but it's not necessary.'

'Please let me be the judge of that. I want to help give Emmie the chance to better herself.' He looked into Lizzie's eyes.

'Now don't go getting offended. I know what kind of money she'll be earning here. I've got a tidy sum in the bank and I'd like to give some to you so you can use it, whichever way you think fit.'

Lizzie frowned.

'Do you believe she could do better for herself than being kitchen maid in a country house, kind as her employers are?' Alfred asked.

'Of course. She's a bright girl. I've been teaching her what I can, but I can't give her my job, now can I?'

'Certainly not. But with you training her and me providing the cash for her to travel and stay somewhere respectable when she has interviews lined up, she'll stand an excellent chance of obtaining a position in a London hotel.'

Lizzie hesitated.

'But she's still so young.'

'Emmie's seventeen. She understands the importance of good food and she has a flair for dessert and sweetmeat making. If she's keen to enter the catering trade, it's high time she became apprenticed.'

'I know I said I'd not stand in her way, but I hate to think of her all alone in London.'

'She'll be working with other youngsters finding their feet. She'll make friends, don't you fret. And if she lands a job at an establishment right in the heart of things, well, his lordship's town house is where I spend a lot of my time.

'I know plenty people working around the West End. With your permission, I'd be glad to keep an eye on her. Take her out to tea now and then. Between Emmie and me, we could keep you posted about her progress.'

'You'd write letters to me?'

He swallowed.

'I could write the kind of letters I

used to dream of writing to you, Lizzie, all those years ago in Canada, far from home and learning how to survive those snowy winters.'

★ ★ ★

Rupert bit his lip.

'Luckily it's not snowing. That really would have been most unpleasant for Velma.'

'You're a kind man, Rupert,' Eleanor said. 'Plenty of people in your position would have tried to shame her, despite her royal connection.'

'Rather a shaky connection to Austrian nobility, but at least you know all the pieces of the jigsaw now. I might have known Steadman would spill the beans.'

'For some reason, he seems to have taken to me. I hope you won't be too cross with him.'

'I shan't. I never could see the point of being vindictive, Eleanor, whoever might have it in for me. Steadman is steady as his name suggests but I'm afraid the Honourable Velma might be tempted to blacken my name. She'd better not try the same trick with you, though!'

'I'm sure people who really care about you won't take a scrap of notice. As for Alfred, what a treasure that man is. What true loyalty he showed this evening.'

'Yes, indeed. Obviously, we could do without more gossip reaching the Press, and he certainly saved me from a sticky situation.'

'If I were Velma, I'd keep jolly quiet about everything. She can only make herself look foolish, don't you think?'

'I suppose. And I'm very glad you are who you are and not Velma. I sincerely, hope I never need to see her again.'

'I doubt you can avoid that, with your wide social circle. Best to keep your dragon slayer close by, don't you think?'

He chuckled.

'He'd appreciate that remark! You're

such fun to be with, Eleanor.'

'I can't help thinking, if her ladyship had turned up and found you ready and willing to let bygones be bygones, she'd have cut a very romantic and glamorous figure in the gossip columns. She is very beautiful.'

'On the surface maybe. I can't believe the nerve of the woman but let's forget her now. I'm relieved you understand the reason why I've been viewed as such a rascal.'

Eleanor avoided his eyes. She sat back and stared at the toes of the white satin slippers peeping from her gown's rosy folds.

'I never thought the day would come when I'd be glad to borrow a pair of my mother's shoes.'

'You look so stunning I doubt anyone with eyes in their head will have given your footwear a second glance.'

'Thank you. I need to tell you I'm sorry for my chilly manner towards you. Especially as you were so kind to me on Christmas Eve.'

'No-one could blame you for having felt affronted.'

'I was relieved to hear the truth, but it's a lesson to me not to heed gossip.' She hesitated. 'It would have been lovely to dance with you tonight, Rupert. I doubt there'll be another chance.'

'Please don't say that. Now you know the truth behind my so-called disgraceful behaviour, I hope we might become friends. There's not that great a distance between our fathers' estates, you know.'

'I know we inhabit different worlds.' She stared into the fire.

A dozen or so people still lingered, chatting and drinking at the other end of the room, though the dancing was finished and most guests had gone home.

'I don't understand.'

'I surely don't need to spell it out. My family has no noble ancestors. My father's money results from years of calloused hands and building up small workshops into big factories. That's

146

allowed him to buy this house and run the stables.'

'All the more credit to him and to your forebears. I'm not afraid of hard work, Eleanor. Nor can I help being born into a family having an endless line of gloomy portraits lining the walls of the ancestral home.'

He loved watching her smile light up her face.

'Some weekends, I take my turn with the lambing and the harvests, like the estate workers do. I muck out the stables whenever I have the time.'

Her eyes widened.

'I never knew that!'

'With respect, you know very little about the real me. I'm no Champagne Charlie. Not like Velma's chum, the aptly named Charlie Bell. I mean no disrespect towards any acquaintance of your family, but that gentleman and my former fiancée are soulmates. Except maybe for the minor detail of his having no title to lay at her dainty hooves.'

Eleanor giggled.

'And I'm no Champagne Charlotte, either. I much prefer horses to people.' She held his gaze. 'But I think I'd enjoy dancing with you. Especially if it was something lively.'

'I'd better warn you in advance that the Charleston defeats me. But you must have many beaux queuing up in hopes of finding favour. I'm well aware you're regarded as one of the most admired debutantes of last year's group.'

'Is that what you've heard? What rubbish. How would any of them know what I'm really like? All those balls and parties and fussing and flirting — mere froth, in my opinion.'

Rupert had to restrain himself from going on bended knee and proposing. He mustn't rush her, even if he was rejoicing at discovering such a precious gem but he couldn't resist taking her hand in his.

'Your parents made me welcome at a time when I wished to spare my own family embarrassment. Maybe you'll at least accept my invitation to luncheon sometime soon? Not until after your return to full health, of course.'

Her gaze dropped to their joined hands.

'That would be very nice indeed.' She looked up again. 'Depending upon the weather in the New Year, don't you think?'

'I'll need to return to my office before too much longer, but please leave the arrangements to me, Eleanor. I enjoy arranging surprises, even if I do possess a pea-like brain!'

'Why on earth do you say that?'

He rose. Walked over to pluck a mistletoe sprig from a garland on the mantle shelf and moved closer to her again.

'Because I've almost wasted an opportunity.'

He held the mistletoe above her head, took a deep breath and kissed her cheek. She said nothing. Heartened, he kissed her lightly on the lips. She shrank back swiftly.

'Are you angry? I didn't mean . . . '

'No, Rupert. I'm not angry, but my mother has realised we're alone so better be prepared for her to come over and coo. I suspect you must meet many mothers hoping to make a good impression.'

He concealed the mistletoe behind a cushion, his lips twitching.

'Not for a while actually. But I understand what you're saying. Sophie has already impressed me as being a thoroughly nice person but not, of course, as much as her daughter has.'

★ ★ ★

Over a leisurely breakfast next morning, Rupert asked Eleanor if she'd like him to give her horse a good gallop.

'Oh, I do so wish I could ride her myself.' Mr Lansdown rustled his newspaper and peered over the top.

'You know that's still impossible, my dear. You should be grateful. Rupert is kind enough to offer when the lads are busy preparing my horses.'

'I am grateful, Pa. Thank you, Rupert. I'd appreciate your giving Stella another gallop.'

Rupert winked at her once her father retreated behind his copy of 'The Times'.

'Think how appreciative Aunt Hester is for all that reading aloud you've done.'

She nodded. This wasn't going to be easy, but she knew she must be ruthless, for both their sakes. She'd spent most of the previous night thumping her pillow and turning on to her other side.

Rupert smiled at her across the table and for moments she forgot everything else in the world that was disturbing her thoughts.

But swiftly she told her stupid heart not to beat so fast when she was trying to be ladylike and sensible. It was ridiculous to feel so happy in his company yet so desolate to think of him leaving next day for London.

Eleanor told herself he'd volunteered a vague luncheon invitation out of politeness and to make amends for his valet taking her name in vain. Soon he'd be on his way in his shiny red Bentley.

She'd known this man a matter of days, during which she'd spent most of the time disapproving of him. Why did she feel so bereft when she knew her crush on Rupert must never go further?

She barely responded when her mother arrived at the table. Rupert chatted with Sophie Lansdown while Eleanor wondered which top-drawer debutante prowling London's ball-rooms and restaurants would be the lucky girl who'd win his heart.

He was unlikely to remain single long, especially should the Honourable Velma's betrayal become known. He'd soon forget the unsophisticated young daughter of the wealthy businessman who'd helped him out of an awkward situation.

'Penny for your thoughts,' Rupert murmured.

'I'm sorry. I thought you were talking to my mother.'

'As you can see, she's left the table. Gone to read her mail, I think. Your father's heading for the stables, which is where I'm off to soon.' His blue eyes showed his concern. 'I'm delighted your parents are content to leave us alone together, but you seem so far away — so troubled. I hate seeing you like this.'

She didn't know what to say. How could she possibly convince Rupert that, despite last night's fireside chat, their budding romance could never blossom?

'I thought we were friends, Eleanor. Last night, I so enjoyed our conversation and I dared to hope you were enjoying my company, too. Please tell me why you seem so distant now? Was it that you regret our kiss beneath the mistletoe?'

She felt tears sting. Angrily, she

shook her head.

'I'm trying to be realistic about you and me, Rupert.'

'Whatever do you mean? Actually, I've decided it best to return to London this afternoon, but it's not as if I'm sailing for America!'

You can't wait to get away, she thought. That's just as well, because it's far too soon for you to begin a friendship with another silly girl.

'Will you permit me to leave my address and telephone number with you? Eleanor? Please answer me.'

Still the right words refused to come. Last night, when he mentioned seeing her again, she'd been flattered. Intrigued. Excited. Not long after, she'd woken from an uneasy sleep, doubt poking inside her head like an icy, probing finger. Now she couldn't even excuse herself from the table and escape upstairs, because of her stupid, stupid weak ankle.

'Do you still wish me to exercise Stella? Shall I go to the stables now?

Will I see you at luncheon?'

'Yes, Whenever it's convenient. But I'm not sure I'll feel well enough to come to luncheon, Rupert. Please forgive me but I'm not myself this morning.'

He rose.

'Let me summon Steadman to help you to your room.'

'Thank you, but I can manage stairs now. I came down alone this morning.'

Eleanor knew the perceptive Alfred Steadman would suspect something and the last thing she wanted was to burst into tears.

But for her father's money, she could well be working alongside the valet as a parlour maid in some big house, or even as a governess if she'd managed to get herself enough learning.

Alfred might be able to subdue scheming society girls but he couldn't smash down class barriers. Without blue blood running through her veins, she'd been a fool even to dream of a future with the young viscount. Eleanor flinched at the thought of what his parents would say about such a union. So why risk heartache by pretending otherwise?

She pulled herself together.

'Thanks again, but on second thoughts, Rupert, I think I shall sit here a while longer on my own.'

'Well, that's told me, hasn't it? All right, Eleanor. Whatever you think best. If I've offended you in any way, please accept my sincere apologies. It won't be long before I'm out of your hair.' He left the room without even a backward glance.

Eleanor put her head in her hands. If he was upset, it could only be hurt pride. But her feelings for Rupert, so unexpectedly kindled on Christmas Eve, would not, she knew, be easily extinguished.

If Only . . .

Stella, with Rupert in the saddle, cantered from the stable yard and down the drive. The lad called Tommy had recommended crossing over the road to follow a bridle path having beautiful views.

Rupert, once astride the horse and grasping the reins, felt his tension ease. How stupid he had been. Eleanor was far too young and newly fledged in society to realise how, with her intelligence, her wit and beauty, she'd make most upper-class young women of his acquaintance seem like painted dolls.

Despite learning how Velma had wronged him, Eleanor was bound to have doubts over a friendship with him. If only she knew his true feelings. If only she knew she need feel no uncertainty about her background, if indeed that was her fear.

His former fiancée always boasted about her royal connections but she'd proved how fickle she was. He knew very little about Miss Eleanor Lansdown, but he knew which one he could trust.

For sure, women were unfathomable creatures and he still couldn't understand what had happened between last night and this morning to return Eleanor to the same cool civility she'd treated him with after he introduced himself on Christmas Eve.

There was no point in trying to coax her into a more cordial state of mind. He had business to attend to in London and it really shouldn't be left unattended for much longer. He also needed to visit his parents and explain to them why their only son appeared to have behaved in such a cavalier manner.

He and Stella were wandering through woodland now. Beyond the trees he saw a stretch of water gleaming in the winter sunshine. He'd take a turn around the lake before heading back then after luncheon, he and Steadman would say their good-byes and drive away from Starminster Manor. The Christmas interlude ended here.

★ ★ ★

'His lordship intends setting off after luncheon, but I can't finish packing until he returns and gets changed.'

'You can eat with me soon as the desserts go into the dining-room.'

Alfred nodded.

'Thank you, Lizzie. I can complete the packing by then. But first I want to give you this.' He held out his hand. 'I've written down the addresses and telephone numbers of my London residence and that of the family seat.' He winked.

'Get away with you!' But Lizzie tucked the envelope in her apron pocket. 'Thank you. I don't suppose you've seen Mr Jeffers lately?'

'Not since breakfast. Shall I look for him?'

'It mightn't be a bad idea. The master might've asked him to tinker with the Rolls Royce and Mr Jeffers has been known to lose track of time. We don't carry a big staff, as you know. It's important he gets his meal promptly, specially with the viscount having his last meal with the family.'

'Leave it with me, my dear.'

Alfred Steadman was in no hurry to leave Starminster Manor. He enjoyed London and was partial to music halls and picture houses in his time off, but having been reunited with Lizzie, he didn't relish leaving her behind for the second time in their lives.

He was also anxious to gain Emmie's confidence. He'd had very little to do with her over the festive period and didn't yet know how her mother intended explaining how she could suddenly afford to buy smart travel clothes, let alone pay for train tickets and accommodation. But first he had an errand to carry out.

The Rolls Royce was kept beneath a lean-to at the far end of the stables. As soon as he glimpsed the car's rear, Alfred called out in dismay and began running, just as Tommy came into the yard, already reaching in his pocket, Alfred suspected, for the makings of a cigarette.

'Tommy! Over here!'

'Where's the fire, Mr Steadman?'

'Quick, lad. It's Mr Jeffers. See?'

'Oh, blimey.' Tommy sprinted the remaining distance, skidding to a standstill beside the butler. He dropped to his knees. 'He's unconscious, but breathing, Mr Steadman. He'll take some lifting, I fancy.'

Alfred crouched beside the pair and tried to find a pulse.

'Yes, thank the Lord. Mr Jeffers? Can you hear me?'

'Cripes,' Tommy said as they waited for a response.

'How far away is the family doctor?'

'He lives down in the village.'

'I'll stay with Mr Jeffers while you get

someone to phone. Come straight back and help me move our friend on to the back seat of the Bentley then I'll drive it round to the front door.'

'I'll shout for Will on the way. Three's better'n two.'

Alfred saw the butler's eyelids flicker and open.

'Mr Jeffers, can you hear me?'

The butler groaned.

'My leg . . . I slipped on an oily patch. Must have fallen awkwardly.'

'Tommy's gone to get help. But we can't leave you on that stone floor. You'll freeze — now keep awake, man, do!' Alfred shrugged off his jacket and placed it over Mr Jeffers, who groaned but managed to whisper his thanks.

Alfred's quick thinking resulted in one very puzzled viscount as Rupert, trotting back into the stable yard, caught a brief glimpse of his beloved Bentley, driven by his valet, pull up at the front entrance to the house.

Despite his dejection, the viscount, seeing only a bulky shape bundled upon

162

the car's back seat, couldn't fail to find humour in the situation.

'Crikey,' Rupert said to the horse. 'What on earth is Steadman up to? For a moment I wondered if he was eloping with the cook!' He groaned. 'I wish your mistress would elope with me, Stella. But there's as much chance of that happening as there is of me travelling to the moon.' He patted the mare's neck.

Steadman got out of the car.

'I'm afraid Mr Jeffers has had a bad fall, my lord. We need to get him inside.'

Rupert slid from the saddle as Tommy and Will arrived together.

'If one of you would kindly see to Stella, I can help with Mr Jeffers.'

'Thank you, sir. I think he's passed out again.'

★ ★ ★

Eleanor, unsure whether she dreaded or yearned for Rupert's imminent departure, arrived in the dining-room, knowing her absence from luncheon would provoke unwelcome interest from her mother.

She allowed her concentration to wander while the others discussed the implications of Mr Jeffers being laid up with a broken leg in the cottage hospital. Then a remark from Rupert penetrated her gloom.

'If I may make so bold, I've come up with a simple solution.' Rupert rested his knife and fork. 'I intend leaving my man with you.'

'We couldn't possibly hear of you doing such a thing!' Edward Lansdown looked at Rupert as though the viscount had suggested taking over the role himself.

'You certainly can, Edward. Steadman is well accustomed to acting as valet, butler, footman and chauffeur — in fact he can probably stand on his head for an encore! Rest assured I'll manage until you're able to make other arrangements.'

'Are you absolutely sure, my boy? It's

an amazingly generous offer.'

'I shall never forget your kindness, taking a total stranger in for the holiday. Besides, Steadman will probably enjoy a break from me. I have a cook who comes in sometimes when we hold a dinner party, or I can stay at my club if it comes to that.'

'Well, if you're quite certain, my boy. From what we know of him, I'm sure Mr Steadman will be perfect.'

'Might I enquire whether your lordship has asked whether he's happy to stay on?' Eleanor focused her stern gaze upon Rupert.

'Eleanor, really!' Her mother frowned at her.

'That's all right, Sophie.' He looked across at Eleanor. 'I can assure you, Miss Lansdown, I've already consulted my valet and obtained his agreement to the arrangement.'

Hearing that chilly 'Miss Lansdown' hit Eleanor like a snowball in the face, even though she'd been equally frosty with him.

Rupert turned back to his host.

'As you know, I shall be bidding you farewell after luncheon. When you've secured another butler from the agency, Steadman can travel back to London by train and join me at my town house whenever you and he are satisfied it's convenient for him to leave.'

'We're all most grateful, Rupert.' Edward Lansdown beamed at his guest. 'I'll come and see you off when you're ready. In my opinion, you're wise to get on the road if you really must leave us.

'I think that snow everyone keeps talking about, might actually reach us later.'

Eleanor's appetite had vanished. But who could blame Rupert for wanting to escape? He seemed to have enjoyed his stay — apart from when Velma arrived and angered him — but he must still be questioning the return of Eleanor's chilly attitude.

If only he realised how she was putting up her defences only to shield herself and him from humiliation and heartache in future. She needed to be cruel to be kind.

Somehow, she got through the rest of the meal, excused herself from drinking coffee and took refuge in her room, where a coal fire burned brightly in the grate.

Rupert had risen and extended his hand in polite farewell. That had been so very hard to bear. Her resolve had almost crumbled. She'd so nearly begged him to stay longer.

Now she sat, gazing at the wintry garden and scolding herself for her stupidity. She saw a few snowflakes drift from the leaden sky but took no notice whatsoever, so intent was she on trying to analyse her recent behaviour, trying to persuade herself she'd acted for the best.

The events of Christmas Eve and the following days had proved she lacked maturity and possessed little or no common sense. She'd condemned Rupert for behaving badly without for one moment considering there might be another side to the scandalous gossip.

Even when deciding to distance herself, she'd been pleased enough for him to ride Stella to hunt. She'd taken advantage of his good nature and her cheeks burned as she recalled incidents, chance remarks, all of which must have convinced him of her stupidity and shallowness.

Last night, as they sat together, chatting at the fireside, she'd felt happier than in ages.

But maybe the demons disturbing her night's sleep were a good thing. Maybe Rupert would decide a bachelor existence was the life for him, given his recent experiences. If it hadn't been for that bird spooking her horse and causing her to fall from the saddle, she'd never have met Rupert before she knew his identity.

He'd been a kind stranger who happened to be driving past in time to help a lone female at the roadside. An image of the good-looking young man gazing down at her, blue eyes showing his concern, while he grasped the horse's reins, popped straight into her mind. She wasn't sure how long she'd been sitting there when she heard sounds of movement outside.

Eleanor got up and peered cautiously around the curtain, only to see Rupert, wearing his overcoat, woollen scarf wound around his neck and a pair of yellow driving gloves, bidding farewell to her father while Alfred gave a last polish to the already shiny car head-lamps.

Whether by fate or by instinct, she didn't know. But something made Rupert look up just as she took in the full scene. Their gazes locked. A frisson of shock passed between them like an electric jolt, and as if there was no thick pane of glass and several yards separating them.

He barely acknowledged her, except as Alfred Steadman opened the driver's door, and before he slid behind the wheel, Rupert gave her the ghost of a smile, leaving her miserable and wondering.

Out in the Cold

Alfred hurried to the rear of the house and deposited his chamois leather and duster in the boot room. As Edward Lansdown had requested, he was prepared to present himself in the master's study in the company of Lizzie Potter.

He found his sweetheart sitting beside the kitchen range staring into space instead of studying the recipe book she held in her hands. To his delight, she looked up, her expression brightening as he appeared.

'I thought you were leaving straight after luncheon, Alfred?'

'I'd never have driven away without saying one last goodbye, Lizzie. In a nutshell, his lordship's left me behind to help you out while a replacement for Mr Jeffers is found. I've been requested to accompany you to the study to meet

171

with Mr Lansdown. I hope that's convenient for you?'

Her mouth became a wide O of surprise. He thought how obedience must be ingrained in her soul as, without hesitation she rose and untied her apron strings. But her fumbling fingers betrayed her nervousness, making him long to help her.

'I have no idea what's going on, Alfred Steadman, but if this is your idea of a joke, you'll never hear the end of it!'

He chuckled, but caught his breath on seeing the expression in her eyes. There was pleasure there, mixed with concern. Without her apron, she looked as he'd seen her at the servants' Christmas meal — a neat, attractive woman resisting middle age with the aid of her sense of humour and trim figure. But he hated to think she might be worrying.

'Lizzie, love, we're not going to the gallows, you know. Your employer merely wants to explain the situation and make sure we're all rowing in the same direction, so to speak.'

She nodded, face serious. He daren't take her in his arms, although he longed to do so.

'It's not my place to say anything before the master talks to you. I didn't engineer this, I promise you,' he added.

'It's been a succession of shocks this Christmas. I — I don't mean to seem rude, Alfred.'

'I know you don't. I caught you on the hop, that's all.'

For a moment he thought she might snuggle against his chest but she moved away as a door banged and Emmie came rushing in from the scullery.

'Guess what! Tommy just got back from an errand. Someone told him it's started snowing back down the road and it's already pitching.' She spotted Alfred. 'Oh, dear, aren't you meant to be driving back to London, Mr Steadman?'

'There's been a change in arrangements, Emmie. Your mother and I are on our way to speak with the master. But I'm sorry to hear there's snow around. I hope it won't affect his lordship's journey.'

'We mustn't keep the master waiting, Emmie.' Lizzie smoothed away a tendril of hair that had escaped her cap. 'While I'm gone, could you have a look through the stock? I need to know if we've caster sugar and desiccated coconut left after all that sweetie making. Could you make a list of things we need to buy, please?'

She turned and sailed towards the door, leaving Alfred to smile apologetically at Emmie before following. Alfred followed her along the corridor and Edward Lansdown quickly opened his study door after the valet tapped on it.

'Come and sit down, both of you. Mrs Potter, you take the easy chair.'

The cook sat down on the chintz-covered seat and clasped her hands in her lap.

'Thank you, sir.'

Mr Lansdown waited for the newest

174

addition to his staff to seat himself before moving behind his desk.

'Please don't look so concerned, Mrs Potter. This is merely a chat to work out how best we can rub along while Mr Jeffers is out of action.'

Alfred saw the relief flooding Lizzie's face and hid a grin. He'd be sure to tease her for not accepting his own reassurances.

'I imagine it'll be some while before we get our butler back again, sir?' she said.

'Unfortunately, you are quite right, Mrs Potter. Too long for us to do without his able services unaided, but I'm delighted Mr Steadman here has kindly offered to help us out — at the suggestion of the viscount.'

'But how will his lordship manage without him all that time?'

'Ah, well, come Monday morning, I shall be in touch with a domestic agency with a view to engaging a temporary man. With luck, we shall only delay Mr Steadman a short time.'

'That's a pity! I was wondering if . . . I mean, that's good. Yes. Good that the viscount won't be inconvenienced for too long.'

Alfred Steadman stared at the tips of his shiny black shoes. Could she have been wondering if he'd be around longer? Even hoping he was somehow wangling his way into the household? He longed to ask her. Such a reaction could influence any decisions about his future. He willed himself to maintain his composure.

Edward Lansdown picked up his fountain pen and twirled it between his fingers.

'Yes, indeed. We're very fortunate to have the help of such an experienced employee.' He leaned forward, put down the pen, and placed both hands palms down upon the desk.

'Everyone will need to be a little flexible. More than usual, I should say. And until the new fellow arrives, I'm relying on you two good people to, shall we say, run the show? How does that sound, eh? Do you think you can work together and bring the best out in the men?'

'And the women too, sir. Pardon me for saying.'

Edward Lansdown looked at his cook and chuckled.

'My apologies, Mrs Potter. For a moment there, I must have imagined I was back in the Army.'

★ ★ ★

Rupert squinted through the windscreen. Wretched weather! He'd dismissed the sullen sky as a warning of rain on the way and Steadman had put up the Bentley's hood ready for the journey.

Rupert had been surprised to find the road beyond Starminster already carpeted in white and now heading towards Gloucestershire, he realised the car's windscreen wipers were struggling to withstand the onslaught of thick feathery flakes.

He hoped this was only a short storm and that when he headed further east, his journey would become easier. No other motorists were braving the elements. Should he turn around and return to the manor house? Try again tomorrow? Rupert felt sorely tempted. But could he cope with the inevitable reaction of Eleanor?

She had made her feelings clear and he still stung at the memory and couldn't understand the reason for her dramatic change of feeling towards him. Presumably despite her knowing the circumstances of his broken engagement, Rupert was still out in the cold.

He smiled wryly, thinking how appropriate that description was at the moment. He was kitted out for Arctic conditions, but the thought of progressing mile after mile, only to find a steep hill rearing ahead like some treacherous white-coated beast, filled him with frustration and no little unease. He'd driven five miles or so.

Ahead of him, the road sloped sharply downwards. Rupert, feeling the car veer from side to side, steered towards the verge, slowing and completing his descent without hurtling too hastily through icy confetti. He managed to steer the Bentley until the motor car sat on the verge, tilting a little towards port, but safely off the main highway.

He switched off his engine. Already, heaped snowflakes partly obscured the windscreen. What a pickle! He hadn't bargained for this. Nor could he recall how far the next town or village might be. Even then, unless he could find a hotel or police station, he didn't think much of his chances. Even a night in a cell was more tempting than a night on the back seat of the Bentley.

Rupert smacked his hand on the steering wheel and wondered how he could have been so stupid as to set off, especially alone, because of a young woman who'd claimed his heart so completely.

Alfred peered through the kitchen window.

'It's settling with a vengeance. I wish I knew whether it was only local or not.'

'You're thinking of his lordship?'

'Of course. I can't help worrying.'

'Maybe he's stopped somewhere,' Lizzie said. 'You know what the upper classes are like. He could be sitting in some hotel, in front of a log fire and snug as a bug in a rug.'

'I can't recall seeing any hotels on that stretch of road. By my reckoning, he can't have driven more than five or six miles.'

Lizzie frowned.

'The next village has an inn. It's probably six or seven miles from Starminster, down a steep hill. You wouldn't notice the inn from the main road but there is a sign pointing to the turning.'

'If he's got that far, I hope his lordship will think to telephone Mr

Lansdown so we know he's all right. If he doesn't, it'll be a big worry.'

Lizzie crossed the kitchen floor to join him by the window. He felt her fingers squeeze his hand.

'You could speak to the master about your concerns. He could telephone the inn, or he could ring the police station at Starminster. They should know about road conditions.'

He turned to face her.

'That's a good idea. I think I should try to do something, Lizzie. There's nobody expecting him back in London and I wouldn't mind betting, if he hasn't found somewhere to shelter, he'll be feeling like a boat afloat on a strange sea, with no lighthouse to guide him.'

'Then you must try and make sure he's safe.'

★   ★   ★

Eleanor put down her book. She'd begun reading 'Carry On, Jeeves' after her mother gave her a copy for

181

Christmas. She couldn't help musing how Alfred Steadman possessed some of the fictional valet's qualities, but even the light-hearted prose couldn't help her from feeling so empty.

After all her protests about not being interested in finding a husband, she now knew how silly she must have sounded. Now, the chance of finding true love seemed far, far way, even after meeting someone who appealed to her and who had behaved so well over the few days he'd stayed.

She didn't have the sophistication, or the cunning of the lady who'd worn his ring for such a short time, and nor would she wish to act like the wealthy flappers who lived for the moment.

Now she'd fallen in love with Rupert, she realised the futility of attending social events she viewed as nothing more than marriage markets. And the last thing she wanted was for her mother to insist he might still be viewed as a possible suitor.

Alone in her room, while Rupert

drove away from her, mile upon mile, she wondered why she'd allowed herself to become so distant towards him. He had obviously felt upset, as the original plan was for the viscount to stay several nights in the country before returning to London.

He'd insisted he had business to attend to, but that, she decided, was unlikely. No. She probably wouldn't encounter him again, unless fate caused their paths to cross, but she couldn't think how that might happen. Again, her impetuous nature had taken over and created this unhappy situation.

Eleanor swung her legs so she sat on the edge of her bed. She looked down at her feet and gently prodded around her right ankle. It felt fine. The swelling had vanished. Maybe she could sneak out and give Stella some exercise. It would do both horse and rider good.

She got off the bed and walked over to the window only to gasp in surprise as she saw the winter wonderland outside. While she'd been reading and half-dozing, lulled by the warmth of the coal fire, snow had blanketed the ground, magicking trees and shrubs into white marble sculptures. But not one flake fell now.

She'd be fine. Stella wasn't afraid of snow and nor was her mistress. She walked to the wardrobe and took out jodhpurs and hacking jacket, not bothering to ring for a maid, so elated was she at the thought of escaping the house.

As Eleanor walked downstairs, she felt confident about climbing into the saddle again. But for fear of bumping into either parent, she headed downstairs and along the staff corridor, intending to slip through the door to the yard. Inside the kitchen she found Alfred, dressed for the great outdoors, accepting a Thermos flask from their cook.

'My goodness, you two seem very serious! Is something wrong?'

Alfred turned to face her.

'Miss Eleanor, please pardon my

impertinence, but you're surely not thinking of going out?'

'I'm hoping to take a short ride, Mr Steadman. The snow has stopped. My ankle is better. I don't see a problem, but I'm longing to know who that flask is for.'

She saw Mrs Potter bite her lip. Watched a shadow cross Alfred's usually serene countenance.

'You don't have to tell me,' Eleanor said. 'It's really none of my business.'

'I've just spoken to your father and expressed my concerns over his lordship, Miss. I'm afraid he might be in trouble, because of the snowstorm.'

Eleanor felt as though her heart was being torn from her chest. She stared at Alfred.

'But surely he left straight after luncheon?'

'Precisely, miss. He could have driven only a few miles before being affected by the snow's full impact. Your father has been in touch with the police, also with the first hostelry along the route his lordship was following.'

'With what result?'

'None at all, Miss Eleanor. I'm setting off now, to see if he — if maybe he's pulled over and is sheltering in the Bentley.'

'Setting off how? Surely not on foot?'

'Tommy's bringing the horse and cart round.' He gave a wistful smile. 'It appears the old ways are sometimes the best, miss.'

'But I can go faster if I ride Stella! I can go ahead of you.'

'I can't allow that, miss. What on earth would Mr Lansdown say?'

'Nothing! Because no-one's going to tell him. Isn't that right, Mrs Potter?'

Cook held Eleanor's gaze.

'If you say so, Miss Eleanor. But please don't delay. You'll need to make the most of the daylight.'

Eleanor nodded and headed for the door, opening it just as Tommy brought the pony and trap round. She smiled as she thought of how Alfred had described this means of transport, making it sound like something a rag and bone man would travel in.

'I'm saddling up Stella, Tommy. Hope to overtake you soon!'

'Cripes. Well done, Miss Eleanor.'

She hurried off to the stables. At least someone thought she had the right idea. And Mrs Potter probably had an inkling of how Eleanor was feeling. After all, the cook had known her since she was a small girl.

Stella seemed glad to see her mistress. She whickered and tossed her mane as if saying it was time to have some fun. Fred, hurrying to check what was going on, helped Eleanor prepare her horse and finally, to provide a leg up into the saddle.

She smiled down at him.

'Thank you, Fred. Wish us luck.'

'All the luck in the world, miss. I'll be waiting for you when you come back with his lordship.'

Only a Heartbeat Away

Rupert, huddled beneath the tartan rug Steadman always kept neatly folded upon the Bentley's back seat, scolded himself for setting off in such a casual fashion. Why hadn't he used his common sense and set off straight after breakfast? Eleanor had made her attitude painfully clear by then.

He could have been safe at home by now, warm and comfortable, instead of trapped in his car, for whose shelter he was of course thankful, but he hated feeling so vulnerable and reliant on help that might or might not arrive.

But the countryside looked beautiful in white. Now the snow had stopped falling, daylight bounced off the dazzling landscape, making him think about getting out and start walking in the hope of finding a farmhouse.

He wondered whether anyone was

thinking about him. His parents must still believe he'd behaved badly and assume he was holed up with friends.

Well, he was certainly falling in plenty of potholes in the course of returning to a life that no longer included Velma. His heart hadn't been broken as easily as his engagement. But if this feeling of matters left unfinished meant what he suspected it meant, he'd be living with this awful, bruised sensation for who knew how long? It served him jolly well right for allowing the delightful Eleanor Lansdown to delude him!

At the tender age of nineteen, six years his junior, she was too young for him, of course. What could she know of life outside her comfortable and secure background? To his knowledge she'd never been engaged and now she'd chosen to remain in the countryside, the pool of eligible young men was not exactly wide. How did one learn to play the game of romance if one didn't allow one's emotions to throw the dice?

Rupert, too, lived a privileged lifestyle, but at least he had travelled abroad and returned to begin earning his living. He didn't spend much time on the family estate these days but London life suited him well — or used to. He would do his duty and continue working for his uncle, but as for social life? He'd lost his appetite.

He checked the time by his pocket watch and groaned. Another couple of hours and daylight would dissolve into dusk. The temperature would drop even lower. He needed to make a decision and make it fast.

Eleanor overtook the pony and trap about three miles along the road. She waved as she cantered by, hoping Stella wouldn't want to stop for a chat. Luckily the sky had lost its ominous look and Eleanor thanked her lucky stars for good visibility helping her cover the miles across snowy ground.

Before long, she spotted the shiny red car at the bottom of the hill. She patted

Stella's neck and leaned in to whisper a warning, slowing the mare to a sedate walk down the grass verge and towards the abandoned vehicle.

As the ground flattened out, they trotted towards the car but Eleanor saw no sign of its driver though he must have got out and attempted to clear windows and running boards before setting off.

She dismounted and, clutching Stella's bridle, made for the driver's door, crisp snow crunching beneath her riding boots. The door handle opened and she looked inside to see if Rupert had scribbled a note to say where he'd gone.

She closed the door again and realised there were only two sets of footprints, one belonging to her and the other to Rupert. There were no signs of any other vehicle having come along so he must have gone on foot in an attempt to find help.

She was faced with a decision. Should she wait for the men to arrive or should she follow the footprints marking which way Rupert had set off? Alfred and Tommy would see she'd gone on ahead and if she didn't continue now, she may just as well have stayed at home, reading by the fire.

Eleanor scrambled back into the saddle and urged the mare on. They'd covered only a few yards when she spotted a figure in the distance. Her tummy lurched. Could that really be the viscount walking so slowly, head down and his whole posture suggesting despair?

Her heart told her what, deep down, she already knew. Love and guilt had sent her on this mission and she needed to show how sorry she was. He still didn't turn around, probably because he hadn't heard her approaching along the snow-covered grass verge. At once she called to him, her voice ringing through air as cold and crisp as a crunchy green apple.

Now he stopped and turned to face her.

'Miss Lansdown? Is that beautiful apparition really you?'

'It really is me, Rupert! But for goodness' sake, do call me Eleanor.'

He laughed aloud and hastened towards her.

'Yes, all right, Eleanor. I'll call you anything you wish. You must know how delighted I am to see you, but surely you're not riding on your own?'

She saw the concern on his face as he looked up at her and told herself not to dismount and enter the shelter of his arms, which is what she really wanted to do. This wasn't the time for personal discussions.

Time was far too precious to waste when they were miles from home with daylight minutes ticking away like a malicious metronome.

'Alfred and Tommy are behind me in the pony and trap. You must be frozen!'

'More cross than frozen! Look at the trouble I've caused.'

'We must keep moving, unless you think we should wait in the Bentley.

The men have shovels and sacks so they might be able to dig the car out.'

'I'm not sure if she'll make it up that hill, though I could follow the tyre tracks I left coming down. That wasn't too much fun but I reached the bottom without damage and it's hardly likely anyone will be coming down it, especially with not a lot of light left.'

'We can't just stand here talking. We have to decide what to do.' Eleanor shifted in the saddle and grimaced. Her ankle had probably worked hard enough today though she wouldn't admit it. But Rupert noticed.

'You are an amazing, brave girl, coming to find me. But I'm worried your ankle won't take much more exercise.'

'Don't worry about me.' She raised her chin. 'When the others arrive, we can sort something out.'

'I'm hoping, if we can get the car moving again, Steadman can drive you home, Tommy will deal with the trap and I can ride Stella back before nightfall.'

They approached the abandoned vehicle. Eleanor peered at the road sloping upwards but the only movement she saw came from a flock of starlings hastening home to roost. They soared and dipped in the sky like a black shawl whipped by the wind.

'How far behind are the chaps, do you think?'

'Probably not more than a few minutes away, by now.'

'Why don't you sit in the car while I keep Stella company?'

'I'm wondering whether we should start for home. What if something's happened to them, Rupert? A problem with the pony or a broken axle?' Suddenly, she felt tired and frightened, even with Rupert so close.

'You make a good point. I have a flashlight in the Bentley, and a rug.'

'But you should lock the car.'

'All I care about is getting you home safe and sound and for Alfred and

Tommy not to be in some sort of pickle. I'm concerned that if something's happened, it'll mean a long walk back for us all, unless we come across some sort of dwelling. And you should definitely rest that ankle.'

'All right, but let's wait just a few minutes.'

He opened the rear door as she slid from the saddle.

'I've got Stella. Put your feet up and tuck that rug around you.'

'I'll wind down the window so you can hear what I have to say.'

He shook his head.

'You don't need to say anything.'

'Oh, but I think I do! I've behaved appallingly towards you and I want to apologise for my rudeness and stupidity.'

Rupert smiled as Stella dipped her head as if trying to listen, too.

'I'm not sure if your horse agrees with you or not.'

'I wish you'd take me seriously, Rupert. I'm no longer a schoolgirl.'

'I know that. But you're young and very beautiful and I understand how you must have felt about having me to stay over the festive period — helping to entertain someone whose reputation seemed, shall we say, tarnished?'

'When you brought my horse to me after my fall, I thought you were the nicest young man I'd met in ages.'

'And I thought you were utterly delightful. I'd no idea who you were, but I wished I could get to know you better.'

'Then you introduced yourself and I allowed my stupid perceptions to distance me from you. I can't believe how childishly I behaved.'

'I quite understand why you were so chilly, but it hurt like blazes.'

'I've been very stupid. Twice now.'

'Not half as stupid as I've been over you-know-who!'

'I've seen photographs of her in the society magazines. Is she truly that beautiful? In real life, I mean.'

'I used to think so when I was smitten, fool that I was. It's taken a while, but I know now what true beauty is.'

'Like Stella, you mean?'

'Um, I really meant like Stella's mistress.'

'I wasn't fishing for a compliment!'

'I know you weren't. That's why you're so refreshing. And now you're blushing just a little and you look more beautiful than ever. I keep telling myself I'm the last man you need in your life — someone who everyone sees as a bounder.'

'But don't you see? After Alfred dropped hints about how gentlemanly you'd been towards the Honourable Velma, I began looking at you like I looked at that unknown young man who rescued me on Christmas Eve.'

'So, what happened between Boxing Night and this morning, Eleanor?'

'I woke up in the small hours and couldn't stop trembling. Wondering how I could possibly think for one

moment you'd be interested in someone like me. Especially after I became
so chilly towards you. I'm so very
ashamed . . . '

'But you're not any old someone!
You're Eleanor. You already know I
think you're beautiful and funny and
brave.'

'And the daughter of a nouveau riche
family.' She spoke quietly. 'If there's any
blue blood in my ancestors' veins, it
must have belonged to people born
centuries ago.'

'Ah. Now I understand.' He hesitated. 'Would you believe me if I told
you I couldn't care even one hoot about
your money or ancestry?'

'In the latter's case, the absence of it,'
she muttered.

'Some of my ancestors were black-
guards, Eleanor. How does that make
you feel? Fisticuffs, forgeries and
financial failures ran rife until my
great-great-grandfather broke the
mould and restored some semblance
of respectability to my family.'

She tilted her face upwards, afraid tears weren't far away, but unable to resist.

Gently Rupert nudged the filly, making her shift enough for him to get closer to the open car window. He stooped, edging forward until his lips were a heartbeat away from Eleanor's.

'Hey! Is everything all right, my lord? Thank goodness we've found you.'

Rupert sighed.

'The cavalry's here, Eleanor. Your reputation is safe.'

★ ★ ★

Lizzie Potter ladled hot chicken soup into a bowl and carried it across to Alfred. Eleanor's father had insisted a bottle of wine should be opened.

'Thank you, Lizzie. This is most welcome, I can tell you. Is Tommy not joining us?

'He tucked into his supper while you were all in with the master. He's with the others now, in the sitting-room.'

'I couldn't have done without his help today.'

She helped herself to soup. Alfred cut a slice of bread for her.

'Thank you. I was too anxious earlier to eat with the others.' She held his gaze for moments. 'Tommy's a good boy. I know I shouldn't pump you for information, but I hope Miss Eleanor didn't get a scolding.'

'Between you and me, his lordship saw to that. He couldn't praise her highly enough.'

Lizzie nodded.

'What happened after you found them? Tommy's not much of a narrator!'

'Won't you take a drink with me? You know Mr Lansdown keeps an excellent cellar?'

She smiled.

'I know, and I'll take a small glass to keep you company, Alfred.'

He poured a little wine for her.

'When we came upon the scene, his lordship said they were trying to decide what action to take. Miss Eleanor's ankle was beginning to trouble her and he wondered if they should start climbing that confounded hill and hope to meet us coming in the other direction.'

'They wouldn't have known about that track Tommy knows, to avoid tackling the hill.'

'That's right. The lad said it was safer than chancing our luck on such a treacherous slope.'

'I suppose his lordship and Miss Eleanor could always have huddled up together in the back of the car for warmth.'

'What, horse and all?'

She giggled.

'I suppose they'd have had a problem squeezing Stella in. I reckon it's a good job you and Tommy arrived when you did.'

Alfred nodded.

'I know I can say this without it going any further. I have the feeling something's been kindled between a certain two persons.'

Lizzie swallowed some wine, coughed and fumbled for a handkerchief.

Alfred got to his feet and rushed round to pat her on the back.

'I'm sorry if what I said shocked you.'

'Please don't let me interrupt your supper. I'm still breathing — it's just that I thought the same thing myself, soon as Miss Eleanor decided she was going to help find his lordship.'

He didn't move away, but placed his hands on her shoulders.

'Can I — dare I possibly hope for something to have kindled between you and me, Lizzie?'

She put her hands up to meet his, then stood up too.

'Surely you don't have to ask me that, Alfred? Maybe it never really faded away in the first place.'

It Had to Be You

Mr and Mrs Lansdown were already taking coffee in the drawing-room when Rupert and Eleanor ate dinner, with the young footman waiting upon them. Rupert waited for apple pie and custard to be served and for the two of them to be left alone before getting a few things off his chest.

'Who'd have thought I'd be back again, having set off all those hours ago. I still feel embarrassed about causing such trouble.' He sighed. 'I shouldn't be surprised if my father disowned me a second time!'

'Once he knows the full story, I think he'll be very proud of you.'

'One can only hope.' He smiled at her.

'I don't even know if you have brothers or sisters.'

'One sister, married and living in

Cheshire,' Rupert said.

'Older or younger than you?'

'Older by several years. I must have been a surprise.'

'Your parents would have been thrilled to have a son and heir, and you know it! I can't imagine you being disinherited as a result of letting everyone think you were the guilty party.'

He shrugged.

'I expect you're right.'

'Anyway, who did your sister marry?'

'Catherine became the Duchess of Bailsford.'

Eleanor put down her spoon.

'You see! I knew I was right.'

'What about?'

'About me not being good enough for your family.'

'What rubbish! With respect, of course.' He grinned at her.

She knew this problem would hang over them like a dark cloud if they didn't address it.

'Rupert, you know I can't compete

with girls like your sister?'

'There's no competition between you and those empty-headed girls who drift from party to party and have to be seen in all the right places.

'Luckily my sister was always out on the farm with me and my father and she married someone who has a big estate. It wouldn't be right for me to propose to you, but now that I've found you, Eleanor, I never want to let you go. I have a plan, but I need to know how you feel about me.'

'We hardly know one another.'

'That's what your father will say, too, but we can soon change that. I fear he won't consider me suitable as a son-in-law, though.'

'You know that's not true. He knows all about the Velma business and I heard him tell you he thought you displayed great fortitude, having heard Alfred's version of events.

'It's not you who's the problem, darling. I wish I could make you understand how shocked your family

206

and friends would be at the thought of me being the prospective bride of a viscount.'

'I shall treat that remark with the contempt it deserves. They can't fail to adore you, though I don't want anyone else falling in love with you except me. And Steadman, if you know what I mean.'

She chuckled.

'Most importantly, you just called me darling. How can I sit here, eating my pudding, when the girl I love calls me darling? Coming from you, that's almost the same as accepting my proposal.'

'You're so funny, Rupert.'

'Does that mean I have a chance?'

'You truly think your parents would approve of me?'

'But of course! They never took to you-know-who, but understandably they were upset to think of me ditching the girl to whom I was engaged.'

'You should tell them the truth soon. I'm sure they'll be very relieved.'

'I fully intend telling them after I talk to your father. Though everyone thinks we're unlikely to see a thaw for some while.' He looked across at her. 'You know I'm happy to have extra time with you, but there are things needing to be sorted out.'

'I understand. May I ask a favour?'

'Ask away.'

'Might I have a private conversation with Alfred tomorrow?'

'You want to learn all my awful secrets?' He put down his spoon.

'No,' Eleanor said sweetly. 'But I believe he'll give his honest opinion on how I might be perceived in the circles you move in.'

'I see. Does that mean, if he provides an answer you approve of, you'll say yes to me regarding an appropriate period of courtship?'

She turned her head.

'The footman's coming back. I'd know that tread anywhere.'

'I feel like a character in a spy novel.' Rupert leaned across the table and whispered. 'I'm desperate to know your answer, so my next question will have to be in code.'

She tried to keep her laughter from bubbling up as the servant entered.

'This sherry trifle's delicious. Do you agree, Eleanor?' Rupert was totally straight-faced.

'I do, Rupert.' She took a final mouthful of apple pie and wondered whether the footman would think they'd both completely lost their reason. But Rupert looked very pleased with her answer.

* * *

'Excuse me, Miss Eleanor. His lordship tells me you'd like a word.'

She looked up from the letter she was reading.

'Hello, Alfred, do sit down. My mother's breakfasting in bed today, so I'm borrowing her sitting-room.'

'I trust Mrs Lansdown is not indisposed, miss.' He seated himself on the nearest chair.

'She's had a lot of organising to do, along with several late nights. That's all it is but I'll let her know you were asking after her. I expect you're wondering what this is all about?'

He inclined his head.

'I can't help noticing how his lordship keeps singing a certain popular song. I'm not too sure, but I believe it might be called 'It Had to Be You'.'

'Goodness, Alfred, I do believe you're on the right track.' She felt a surge of joy.

'May I say, I'm very happy to hear it, Miss Eleanor.'

'I think you know I'm happy, too, Alfred.'

'I do, miss, although I sense a 'but' coming.'

'Alfred, how can I possibly allow his lordship to court me when I have no title — no noble background at all?'

'Forgive me for saying so, Miss Eleanor, but that is absolute piffle!'

'Really? I get the distinct impression

his parents are rather, well, sticklers for tradition. As for his sister, she's married to a duke, isn't she?'

Alfred leaned forward, his hands on his knees.

'Between you and me, Caroline was a tearaway. She drove her parents to distraction and broke hearts galore until she met the duke and then — oh, my word, I'm not sure how to put this . . .'

'Surely there wasn't a scandal? No wonder Rupert didn't want to go home after the Velma thing blew up.'

'There was a scandal in the making, miss. The duke rescued her from a potentially embarrassing situation and the two of them fell in love. Suffice to say, the marriage took place with the minimum of fuss, and I'm delighted to report the couple are extremely happy together, with their young family.'

Eleanor sat back.

'I see. So that's why Rupert's parents gave him a hard time when they thought he'd jilted you-know-who? They had a special reason for fearing another scandal in the family.'

'Precisely,' Alfred said. 'His lordship isn't always skilful at defending his own actions even though he is immensely polite and thoughtful of others.'

'And funny.'

'Indeed.'

'But I doubt his parents would find anything much to laugh about in being asked to welcome little Miss Nouveau Riche to their world? Please be honest with me, Alfred.'

He leaned towards her.

'I tell you something, Miss Eleanor. You'll be like a breath of fresh air to that family. You're worth ten of those flibbertigibbets who flatter themselves they're good enough to attract the viscount, just because a drop of blue blood runs in their veins!'

'Alfred, I think I love you.'

'The feeling's entirely mutual, miss.'

The pair beamed at one another.

'Now, may I tell you my own secret?'

'I shall be honoured to hear it, Alfred. And my lips are sealed.'

'I've popped the question to Lizzie Potter and she's said yes.'

Eleanor blinked hard.

'You want to marry the lovely lady who is our cook? But . . . I was going to say surely you've only known her since Christmas Eve?' She coughed. 'I'm a fine one to talk.'

'Between you and me, Miss Eleanor, my Lizzie and I have, shall we say, history. We first met more than seventeen years ago. After I left the country to work in Canada, Lizzie married a good man but she's been widowed a while now.'

'Do you mean you only found her again because of coming here with the viscount?'

'I do, and it was a shock, but also a great delight, to both of us.'

'Well,' Eleanor said. 'That's an amazing story, but I shan't say a word until you announce your engagement.' Secretly she felt envious of Alfred's obvious pleasure and wondered whether her own romantic situation could be resolved, too.

'I'm not sure how things will work out, but I don't intend giving Lizzie up a second time, not after Fate has brought us together again after all these years.'

'No indeed. I suppose this proves the best things in life are worth waiting for.'

Changes on
the Horizon

'I insist you stay and see the New Year in with us, my boy. Apart from the fact that we enjoy your company, the roads won't be safe until then, if the weather forecast's anything to go by.'

Edward Lansdown looked up at his stand-in butler.

'Thank you so much, Steadman. If you leave us that decanter, I think his lordship and I can manage quite well for the rest of the evening. I'm sure you'll appreciate an early night.'

Alfred glanced at his employer, who smiled his agreement.

'Thank you, sir. And my lord. A very goodnight to you both.' He left the room quietly.

'Splendid chap, that valet of yours. Extremely competent.'

'He's a former military man, of course. Keeps me in order without me realising it half the time!'

The older man cradled his brandy goblet in one hand and swirled the amber liquid around.

'You did say you wanted to discuss something with me? Does it concern Steadman? I'll understand if you've had second thoughts about leaving him with us.'

'No second thoughts, sir. What I have to say concerns your daughter,' Rupert said, sitting up straight.

'Look, my boy, if you think you need to buy some little gift because she rode to your rescue, you really don't need to bother. Eleanor's an impetuous girl and she relishes a challenge.'

'She's also courageous and a delight to spend time with. A good horse-woman, too.'

Her father looked heavenwards.

'You might add stubborn to that list, not forgetting the fact that she drives her mother crazy!'

Rupert stopped gazing at the logs burning brightly in the hearth.

'What I have to say will probably come as a surprise, sir.'

'Come now, it's Edward to you, my boy.'

'Of course. Here we go, then, Edward. I would like your kind permission to request your daughter's hand in marriage — only after a suitable time of courtship of course, and without making a grand fuss and kerfuffle, given events in my recent past.'

'Good grief!'

'Regarding that whole wretched business in London, Edward, I can't tell you how grateful I am to you for inviting me here for Christmas and, well, everything really. It goes without saying, I didn't intend falling in love when I turned up on Christmas Eve.'

'No, I don't expect you did.' Eleanor's father blinked hard. 'Do I take it that my daughter is agreeable to this, er . . . courtship?'

'Yes, to my utter delight, she is.'

'Good grief!'

Rupert wasn't sure what to make of that comment coming along a second time but ploughed on.

"To be frank, Eleanor was not without some apprehension at first. I believe she might have found the whole business of my ancestry rather daunting. Can't blame her for that. I'd be put off by that succession of ne'er-do-wells, all of whose portraits grace the ancestral hall!'

'You might find it best not to repeat that opinion of yours if speaking to my dear wife.'

'Ah . . . understood.' Rupert beamed.

'But my dear boy, can we be absolutely clear about this? Are you saying you wish to become engaged to Eleanor after knowing her only a matter of days?'

'Not formally engaged, Edward. I don't want to rush her into anything. I have at least learned a few things from my former unfortunate liaison. What

I'm saying is, we would like your blessing as to the two of us having an understanding.

'I need to clear the air with my parents then carry out certain duties in London, after which, I'd like your permission to come and take Eleanor out for luncheon. Maybe present her with a little keepsake, as a token of my feelings for her. Not a ring just yet but some other item of jewellery perhaps.'

He bit his lip, willing Edward Lansdown not to say, 'Good grief!' again.

'Great Scott! This news comes as an enormous surprise, Rupert.'

'I apologise if I'm speaking out of turn. I suspected my request would startle you, but I'm delighted to know my feelings are reciprocated, so couldn't bear to keep the matter under wraps any longer.'

'It's just that my daughter has always maintained being married isn't the be all and end all. She can be rather scathing about some of the young gentlemen she meets.'

Rupert chuckled.

'She has made her opinions abundantly clear and I must admit I find her so very refreshing. Different. Funny. I feel I've discovered my soulmate and fortunately she seems to feel the same about me. I sincerely hope so, anyway.'

'Well, I'm blessed.' Edward struggled to swallow his mirth.

'I'm sorry to have sprung this on you after such a short acquaintanceship and with my former engagement so recent. Though, I must say my feelings for your daughter are entirely different from those I experienced for the, um, other young lady.'

'Ah, but how am I, and indeed my daughter, to be sure of that?'

Rupert was aware he was making a botch of this. He took a deep breath.

'It's perfectly logical you should be suspicious. I'm well aware Eleanor is only nineteen, while I'm several years older.'

'Which in itself is not a problem,'

Edward assured him. 'Had you known her for longer, I would be more understanding. But after meeting her less than a week ago, you're contemplating a future together, something which until recently you were presumably planning with your former fiancée?'

This didn't bode at all well. Rupert lifted his chin.

'What can I do to reassure you and make you change your mind?'

'Give yourself time, my boy. And Eleanor needs time, too. I took a liking to you right from the first and I understand the Honourable Velma led you a fine dance, with which I fully sympathise.

'But Eleanor is barely out of finishing school. She should meet more young men than she already has. It concerns me how she's formerly pronounced most of them as numbskulls, but out of the blue she's contemplating matrimony with you.' He shook his head. 'You see my point?'

Rupert bowed his head.

'I can't bear the thought of losing her, Edward.'

'If her feelings are as strong as you believe, surely that won't be an option? If I were you, I'd keep quiet about all this and see how you both feel after a period of separation.

'You sound as though you're going to be busy in London as well as on your family estate, so why not enjoy these extra few days with us and come back nearer the spring? Letters and telephone calls will help you keep in touch with each other's doings.'

Slowly Rupert nodded his head, even managing to force his features into a smile, or maybe the ghost of one. But what did he expect Edward Lansdown's response to be?

Any father worth his salt would be protective of his beautiful young daughter, even when a prospective suitor came with a respected title and was presumably solvent, judging by his lifestyle.

In his turn, he respected the man whose son-in-law he wished to become. But the thought of Eleanor attending parties and dances around the county, while the man who loved her kept a low profile, filled him with dismay.

'Thank you for your thoughts, Edward. I think, as soon as the roads are passable, I shall be on my way. Spending Yuletide with you has been most enjoyable but I need to get on with my life now. Build some bridges and hope, when the time comes, you'll feel confident I'm the right man to become Eleanor's husband.'

* * *

'I can't believe you let me sleep in! Surely Rupert didn't need to set off so early? Stupid, stupid, weather — why couldn't it have snowed again?' Eleanor sank on to a chair and glared at the toast rack.

'The snow began to melt last night so when he awoke this morning, he made a swift decision,' her father replied. 'And he really has much to attend to, both at his family home and in London. He asked me to say goodbye to you.'

'But things have changed now. He's told you how we feel about one another, hasn't he, Pa?'

'Indeed he has. I believe the discussion we had was perfectly open and honest.'

She stared back at him.

'Did you send him away?'

'On the contrary, Eleanor. I suggested he stayed over Hogmanay so the two of you could spend more time in each other's company.'

Eleanor felt as though a cold hand was squeezing her heart.

'And he still decided to leave?'

Edward Lansdown looked slightly guilty.

'Eleanor, believe me, I had only your best interests at heart when I suggested too much haste was not a good thing. I told Rupert he was welcome to write to you or telephone but I got the feeling he decided it best to get back to everyday life. I'm sure you'll hear from him soon, my dear.'

'I can't believe you acted like you did!' She kept her voice low, despite her anger. 'That dreadful woman will snap her jaws and get her teeth into him again.'

'If he allowed that to happen, after all he told me about his feelings for you, I would say you'd had a lucky escape, Eleanor. Your comment only serves to prove my point.'

'Which is?'

'That you may be nineteen years of age, but you're acting rather like a spoilt child who can't have what she wants. Have trust in the young man. Allow him to sort out his feelings and his relationship with his parents. Do you really want them to view their son's friendship with you as some sort of rebound romance?'

Eleanor sat back in her chair. She'd never had such a conversation with her father before.

'I see what you mean. They might think of me as someone totally different from the person I really am. Yet another young woman who's trying to get their son in her clutches!'

Her father looked delighted.

'Good girl. Now, that remark shows me you're more than capable of behaving in a mature manner. Let's have some breakfast and discuss our plans for the New Year's racing schedule. You know how much I value your opinion.'

★ ★ ★

'We need to make plans, Lizzie.'

'There's been so much going on round here, I'm not sure I can think straight, Alfred. This is the first evening in weeks I'm cooking dinner for family only. Not counting us lot, of course!'

Alfred nodded. That was why he'd waited until things became quieter, hoping to gain her full attention.

226

'My word, these ginger biscuits are first class.'

'Aren't they? And before you ask, yes, Emmie made them.'

'Which proves she has all the more reason to begin planning her new life.'

'She told me you'd helped her make a list of hotels.'

'It's a good time of year to apply for a post, once the festivities are behind us. Staff often change jobs once Christmas and New Year are over.'

'While I think of it, Mr Lansdown says the agency are sending the new man at the weekend. I expect you know that.'

Alfred gave her a wry smile.

'No. I'm not as important as you are.'

'Flatterer! More likely the master didn't want you buying your train ticket yet. He'll not want to let you go before he has to.'

'Perhaps. However, I do know something that you probably don't . . . '

She sat back in her chair and folded her arms.

227

'I need to put the joint to roast soon. Just marking your card.'

'I can take a hint. The viscount plans to visit the weekend after next. So, if all's well with Mr Jeffers's temporary replacement, I shall be returning to London in the Bentley.'

'I see.' Lizzie looked down at her fingers. 'I suppose it could've been worse.'

'For us or for poor Mr Jeffers?'

'At least we have a little more time together.'

'Lizzie, I don't know whether you've faced up to it, but for us to be together — as in married — you're going to have to leave Starminster Manor.'

She twisted the narrow gold band she still wore on her ring finger.

'I realise that, of course. I'll be sorry to go but if Emmie leaves, there's nothing to keep me here, is there? Not when I can begin a new life with you.'

He felt a huge sense of relief. And happiness.

'Exactly, my dear. I can't wait. But I'd better get on, too. I just wanted to make sure we were thinking along the same lines.' He rose. 'Thank you for the tea. I might know more, once I speak to his lordship about you and me. He may have something in mind.'

'You can't mean he'd take me on, too?'

'I don't know, do I? He might well be considering his own future and he's made it abundantly clear how much he enjoys your cooking.'

'Has Miss Eleanor said anything to you, about you-know-what?'

'All I can tell you is that they're corresponding. She didn't say anything to me this morning when she handed me a letter to post, but in my humble opinion, she has a bit of a glow about her.'

'I can imagine those two making a lovely couple.'

Alfred reached out and touched Lizzie's cheek with one finger. He loved watching her cheeks redden as she looked round to make sure no-one was watching.

'You've known her since she was a small child, haven't you?'

Lizzie nodded.

'Miss Eleanor is two and a half years older than Emmie. She was six when I started here. She had a governess and of course Emmie went to the village school. They played together at weekends. I've always had a soft spot for Miss Eleanor but Emmie never shared her love of horses.'

'That's bound to be a big consideration for Miss Eleanor in terms of whom she might marry and where she might settle.'

'You mean she'd rather live somewhere like this?'

'People have been known to keep horses in London, you know. But we all know the young lady's views on people who exist on a diet of parties. It's fortunate his lordship feels the same.'

'Are you telling me I should look to my wedding cake recipe?'

'Not for some while, I fancy. Emmie will be the one to move first, you mark my words.'

'You know I'll be pleased for her if — when — that happens.'

Lizzie sounded wistful and Alfred wished he could wave a magic wand to make everything slot into place.

'And you'll miss her very much. I'm not that daft. But when I talk about changes, I don't mean only for Emmie and us.'

Six Months Later

Eleanor signed her name at the bottom of the page and screwed the top back on her fountain pen.

My darling Rupert
Thank you for your last letter, which arrived before I had time to answer the previous one. You're such a mystery man! I cannot think why I need to be collected by Alfred and driven to my birthday luncheon, when Jeffers could easily have transported me. It's a pity I cannot drive myself, but I plan to learn, you know.

It will be easier now Mr Jeffers has fully recovered, poor man. Did I tell you he's lost weight and it suits him? Mrs Potter has to hide gingerbread away, so he doesn't fall back into his former bad habits.

But to return to the matter in

hand, I shall do as you request and make sure I'm ready for collection (like a parcel?) at 10 o'clock on Friday morning. Also as requested, I shan't wear anything too flimsy and floaty. On second thoughts, perhaps I should choose jodhpurs and hacking jacket?

My father's a hard taskmaster but I'm enjoying everything I've taken on for him. I'm not trying to make you jealous, but Pa and I were at Newmarket last week and who should we bump into but Charlie Bell!

Then yesterday, when Pa took me to see a brood mare he'd heard about, guess who called to see me? Yes, Champagne Charlie! Mother gave him tea on the terrace and he asked whether I was spoken for. Isn't that frightful? Mother whispered to me that she thought Charlie Bell was putting on quite a bit of weight and had the makings of a double chin! She told him I was spoken for but it must remain a secret. *Apparently, he didn't hang around long after that.*

Well, I'd better finish here if I want to catch the next post. It seems an absolute age since I saw you, dearest Rupert. Friday cannot arrive too soon. Please tell Alfred I look forward to a nice chat in the car.

Toodle-pip!
With all my love,
Eleanor.

Once she'd read through her words, she added a couple of kisses and sealed the single sheet in a cream envelope, addressed to Rupert at his London home. Who'd have thought, months after their first meeting, she and he would still be continuing their friendship even if conducted mainly by mail?

Her father had been so wise although, at first, she resented what she viewed as his quaint approach to her romance.

Back in December, in her desolation, she believed she'd never see Rupert again, but he telephoned as soon as he reached his parents' home and he explained her father's advice, telling her it was entirely reasonable, even though he agreed it felt harsh to them.

He said they needed time to adjust and following that, he'd visited her now and then. On one occasion she travelled to London where Alfred Steadman met her train at Paddington Station and drove her to the viscount's home in Knightsbridge.

His sister was staying, too, making Eleanor feel special because of being invited at the same time. Caroline had been a delightful chaperone to the young couple and Eleanor and her sister-in-law to be were already friends.

But she longed to see Rupert every day of her life. Still seated at the desk, Eleanor closed her eyes, imagining herself crossing a luxurious hotel foyer, her heels sinking into the thick carpet pile as she walked towards him. He'd hold out his arms and whisper, 'Happy birthday' before holding her close.

She opened her eyes abruptly the moment she heard her mother call from the doorway.

'My dear, are you joining me for luncheon, or are you not? You know I have an appointment with my dressmaker at two-thirty and she's coming here as usual.'

She had forgotten. But if she skipped lunch, she could hurry to the village to post her letter so it was speeding on its way as soon as possible. Lovely Lizzie Potter would see she didn't go hungry. She decided she'd better not say anything about Alfred collecting her on Friday, in case he arrived with no time left to visit his fiancée.

Her mother was calling again. Eleanor picked up the letter and went off to make her apologies.

*   *   *

After a hilarious evening with his old school friend, Rupert bid his host farewell and descended the elegant

Regency house's front steps, to find his car. The property, perched on the border between Wiltshire and Somerset, was the perfect place for a rendezvous, especially as Eleanor would have no idea where Alfred Steadman would be taking her. All part of the plan.

His feet crunched on gravel as he headed for the stables. Rupert lifted his hand in greeting when he saw his hired chauffeur crossing the yard, then followed him to the vehicle waiting nearby.

Five minutes later they were bumping along a rutted lane, beyond which lay the field Rupert, over the last months, had come to know well. His trusty henchman guided the black saloon through the gate and stopped alongside the nearby hangar. All Rupert wanted now was for the rest of the arrangements to fall into place as neatly.

'There we are, my lord. I moved Dolly and parked her round the back. She's fuelled up ready to roll. The rest is up to you, sir.'

'Thank you, Mr Cannings,' Rupert

said. 'It certainly is up to me.' He checked his watch. 'They should be here any time now. Weather's looking good, don't you think?'

'Well nigh perfect, I'd say, sir. I shall be back well before five o'clock, ready to assist. Maybe you'd like me to wait, rather than abandon you now?'

'That's very thoughtful of you. I believe Mr Steadman won't be too far away but it would be a comfort to know you're still around.'

'Whatever you say, sir, though I'm satisfied Dolly's in tip-top condition.'

Rupert watched the chauffeur position himself near the hangar before approaching the little aircraft. He walked all around, checking items he knew Mr Cannings had already inspected, wanting everything to be perfect for this, the most significant day of his life so far.

He didn't have long to wait before hearing the purr of his Bentley. Watching it nose its way into the field, Steadman at the wheel, his heart gave what was almost a hop, skip and jump, but Rupert knew very well what, or rather who, was causing this to happen.

'Rupert! How dashing you look! Doesn't he look splendid, Alfred?' Eleanor allowed her beau to help her from the front seat. He knew it would have been most unlike her to sit in solitary state in the rear.

He kissed her hand.

'Happy birthday, darling Eleanor. You look superb in those greens and blues. Like — like an elegant kingfisher!'

'Thank you. I thought culottes and tunic would fit the bill.' She glanced around. 'But why are we meeting in a field? I tried to wheedle some information out of Alfred, but with no success whatsoever. Are we going to have a picnic beside that hangar? I adore picnics, by the way.'

Alfred cleared his throat.

'I'll wait until you, erm, depart, shall I, my lord?'

'That would be fine, Mr Steadman,' Rupert said. 'Then you can drive back to Starminster to see Mrs Potter.' He took Eleanor by the hand. 'Come, Miss Lansdown. Your carriage awaits.'

He watched her face as he led her round the hangar to where the aircraft stood on the close-cropped turf. She looked highly uncertain and for a moment, he feared he might have misjudged his lovely lady's appetite for adventure.

'Rupert? Are we actually going to . . . but where is the pilot? Is he that man standing over there?'

'No, your pilot is here beside you, my love. This is part of your birthday surprise.'

'It's a wonder I'm not already speechless. Dare I ask how many other parts there are to my gift?'

'Two, as it happens, but first let me help you on board.' He took her hand.

'It really is fortunate I chose to wear culottes.'

'You'd have managed, but the culottes are very fetching. Did I already tell you that?'

'No, but nor did you tell me you could pilot a plane.' She put a hand on Rupert's shoulder and climbed through the open door.

'I've been fortunate to have an excellent instructor these last months. I thought it would be a useful skill and one that would please you, my darling.'

'I can't believe this is happening, Rupert, but it's very exciting!'

He made his way to the pilot's side where he began his preparations for take-off. He smiled to himself, still unable to believe his luck that this long-awaited day was here at last. He started up the engine and began to taxi the aircraft towards the track leading to the runway. Mr Cannings gave him a thumbs-up sign and moved off.

'Where are we going?' Her voice rang out above the engine's steady rumble and growl.

'We're going across the water, but don't worry. I'll do my best not to get your pretty feet wet in the Bristol Channel.'

241

'Behave yourself, Lord Colford. I trust you to take good care of me.'

'Hold tight. I'm about to get us airborne.'

Rupert pulled back the stick. Eleanor felt the thrust of the engine pin her back to her seat as the little craft raced along the runway. She gasped in amazement as that magic moment arrived and the aircraft thrust itself off the ground like some exuberant big bird. She laughed out loud as she looked down at treetops and saw the road winding like a grey ribbon below.

Rupert informed her he was watching for his usual landmarks, also keeping an eye on his instruments.

'Everything all right back there?' He called over his shoulder.

'Divine, thank you.'

'This is not a long flight. We'll be eating an early lunch so I hope you're peckish.'

'Peckish? I'm still almost speechless.'

'Only almost? Just you wait, young lady!'

242

It was at that moment she knew she loved Rupert more than she'd realised it was possible to love a man.

Eleanor glued her nose to the window, enjoying a clear view of houses and railway tracks and church steeples. They crossed the Somerset coastline and she exclaimed at the sight of a Victorian pier jutting away from a beach they both agreed they remembered from childhood visits.

They also agreed they weren't quite sure where the River Severn merged with the ocean but they liked the way sunshine turned the sea silver beneath their wings.

'There's a little under nine miles between here and the Welsh coast,' Rupert said. 'You'll be pleased to hear we'll be landing in a field owned by a friend. You'll be doubly pleased to hear I've flown in there several times before.'

'Good. Are we lunching with this friend of a friend?'

'All will be revealed after our arrival.'

243

To the Stars and Back

'Alfred Steadman! What on earth are you doing here?'

'Got a kiss for me? There's nobody looking.' Alfred closed the back door behind him, dumped two overnight bags at his feet and held out his arms.

'Get away with you!' But Lizzie put down her whisk and hurried over to him.

'I've missed you so much, love,' he murmured, holding her tight.

'Same here. It's grand to see you again. But I'm very confused. Miss Eleanor said you were collecting her first thing and driving her to meet his lordship. I assumed I wouldn't see you until you drove her back later.'

'It's a long story. Any chance of a cuppa?'

'Why don't you make us both one while I finish mixing this sponge cake? I

can take a little break then. I've sent
Violet and the new girl out for a breath
of fresh air.'

'I know how much you must miss
Emmie, but you must be pleased she's
doing so well at the Strand.' He was
filling the kettle.

'It's true I miss her, but you and Mr
Jeffers were right about her needing to
move on. She loves her job, as you well
know.' She glanced at the clock.
'There's a birthday dinner for Miss
Eleanor tonight, just a small affair, but I
want everything to be really special. The
master and mistress are lunching with
friends, fortunately.'

'The viscount is, as I speak, no doubt
romancing Miss Eleanor.' Alfred was
fetching two cups and saucers.

'About time too, I reckon.' She
stopped what she was doing and
frowned. 'You brought two bags in from
the car. What's going on, Alfred?'

She continued whisking batter for a
sponge cake while she listened to his
account of the morning's activities,

raising her eyebrows when he mentioned the flight to Wales.

'I couldn't write and tell you because it was all hush-hush. Her father knows, of course.'

'She'll love it, won't she? Such a daredevil that girl is. But flying somewhere just to have their luncheon?' She clicked her tongue. 'I can't believe some of the things posh folk get up to!'

'His lordship may be top-drawer, but d'you remember me telling you he was a man of the people? A while back, I put my cards on the table and told him about you and me needing a position together.'

'Really? And how did that go down?' Lizzie laid a muslin cloth over the cake basin and took a seat beside Alfred.

'It's taken a while to bring all his plans to fruition — his words, not mine — but last night he told me he would like us to run his London house for him. For the foreseeable future and with some outside help where necessary, of course. And, um, not until after we become man and wife, of course. That goes without saying.' He patted her arm.

'Alfred Steadman, are you serious?'

'Perfectly.'

'But what does his lordship mean by 'the foreseeable future'?'

'Ah, now, that's a bit trickier. Think back to that night you and I sat here talking. This is going back to that time his lordship got stuck in the snow.'

'When you prophesied big changes for more people than just us?'

'Precisely. There's one more piece needs fitting in the jigsaw.'

★ ★ ★

'Do you know what I was thinking about, Rupert? When you were flying us across the water?'

'I'm hopeless at guessing, darling girl. How's your grilled lemon sole?'

She leaned towards him.

'Delicious, thank you. Everything's delicious. But what I was thinking was,

247

if you hadn't driven into a snowstorm after Christmas when you were trying so hard to get away from me, today would never have happened.'

'I believe it was Fate taking a hand, Eleanor. I apologise for contradicting you, but I never wanted to get away from you. I fell in love with you as soon as I saw you and your jodhpurs sitting in that mucky ditch. You were the one who drove me away, angel.'

She hung her head.

'I know. And I'm so sorry. I was such a child.' She sighed. 'Another year and I shall become totally grown-up and boring.'

He roared with laughter.

'You could never become boring. But I hope one or two things about you will have changed by the time next June arrives.' He reached inside his waistcoat pocket.

Her eyes widened at sight of a small black leather box.

'Eleanor?' He pushed back his chair and dropped down on one knee. 'Will you do me the immense honour of becoming my wife?' He opened the box and took out a ring. 'Crikey, should I have said please?'

She stared at him, unable to speak for some moments.

'Rupert, darling man — are you quite sure about this?'

'I certainly am. I love you very, very much, my darling.'

'And I love you very much, too. I'm as sure of my feelings as I am about letting you fly me to the moon, if you wished.'

'Not sure Dolly would make it, but I love it that you trust me.' He slid the glittering diamond ring upon her finger then stood up again and smiled down at her.

'Now, why don't I whisk you back to England? There's more to come, my love. Your birthday's not over yet.'

'Aren't you forgetting something?'

Light dawned. He stooped and kissed her very tenderly to a small round of applause from nearby diners.

'There you are, my darling. I've plighted my troth.'

*   *   *

'How lovely that the master invited us in to drink the young couple's health. I must say, it seems strange to think of Miss Eleanor becoming a viscountess.'

'I'm immensely relieved she is, Lizzie. I might've been forced to seek other employment if his lordship had married you-know-who.'

'This way, we can work together for people we respect and care about.'

'Indeed. His lordship has given me permission to tell you one more thing, Lizzie.'

'Is this the missing piece in the jigsaw?'

'It is. There was always the chance Miss Eleanor would decide not to marry his lordship.'

'I'm so glad that didn't happen, Alfred.'

'We both are. But you weren't the

250

only one wondering how Miss Eleanor and the viscount would share their time between London and Somerset. His lordship's parents are both hale and hearty with no desire yet to give up the many duties involved in running the estate.'

'Go on.'

'A decision has now been made.'

'Ooh, this is like waiting for a bus that never arrives!'

'Sorry, love. His lordship tells me a house is to be built upon his father's land. Once all is ready, he and his bride can live in it, as and when necessary. He intends keeping on the London property but Miss Eleanor will become involved with a scheme both of them are keen upon and which Mr Lansdown will take a part in, too.'

'Not flying?'

Alfred chuckled.

'I wouldn't have put it past them, but no, it's horse breeding. In a small way and as a sideline to the Lansdown race horse enterprise. It will link the two families and his lordship knows his bride's father would miss her help.'

'She's not the sort to sit around at tea parties, gossiping about high society.' Lizzie grinned. 'Especially now she's marrying into it.'

'I haven't quite finished. Once the new house is complete, you and I will be spending time in Somerset as well as London. That's the plan, but I need to be sure you approve. It'll be a challenge, but it means you'll still see something of Emmie.'

He held his breath. Lizzie was the missing piece in his own jigsaw.

'Alfred Steadman, it feels like Christmas come around all over again. Being with you and seeing more of my daughter — of course I approve!'

He jumped up as someone tapped before pushing the kitchen door open. Eleanor stood there, smiling at them both. Rupert appeared behind her. Alfred reckoned they both looked as though they'd flown to the stars and back.

'All in order, Mr Steadman?'

'Very much so, my lord.'

'Does that mean I'll still have you around to keep me on the straight and narrow?' Rupert winked at Lizzie.

'Indeed you will, sir. And after years of dealing with Miss Eleanor, may I say I'm just the woman for the job.'

We do hope that you have enjoyed reading this large print book.

Did you know that all of our titles are available for purchase?

We publish a wide range of high quality large print books including:
Romances, Mysteries, Classics
General Fiction
Non Fiction and Westerns

Special interest titles available in large print are:
The Little Oxford Dictionary
Music Book, Song Book
Hymn Book, Service Book

Also available from us courtesy of Oxford University Press:
Young Readers' Dictionary
(large print edition)
Young Readers' Thesaurus
(large print edition)

For further information or a free brochure, please contact us at:
Ulverscroft Large Print Books Ltd.,
The Green, Bradgate Road, Anstey,
Leicester, LE7 7FU, England.
Tel: (00 44) 0116 236 4325
Fax: (00 44) 0116 234 0205

MEDITERRANEAN MYSTERY

Evelyn Orange

Leda unexpectedly finds herself companion to her great aunt on a Mediterranean cruise. Assuming it will be a boring holiday with a crowd of elderly people, her horizons change as she explores the ports of call, and discovers that Aunt Ronnie is lively company. There's also a handsome ship's officer who seems to be attracted to Leda, plus intriguing fellow passenger Nick, who's hiding something. Added into the mix is a mystery on the ship — which becomes a voyage with unforeseen consequences . . .

FIRESTORM

Alan C. Williams

1973: Debra Winters has started a new life for herself as a teacher in a small Australian outback town. Given the responsibility of updating the school's fire protocol, she is thrown together with volunteer firefighter Robbie Sanderson, and there's a spark of attraction between them. Meanwhile, things are heating up: it's bushfire season, and there's an arsonist on the loose. Debra and Robbie find themselves in danger. Will their relationship flicker out — or will they set each other's worlds alight?

A GIFT FOR CELESTINE

Sheila Daglish

The village of St Justin is happy for archaeologist Alex to create a festival exhibition in the chateau beside the Dordogne. The highlight of the display is a fabulous necklace, a gift for a local girl who, centuries ago, was loved by the lord's son. But the jewels bring danger for Alex — and to brooding vineyard owner Raoul. Raw from past betrayals, he denies his attraction to her even as they are drawn closer. But Alex knows there can be no true love, no future, for them without trust . . .

A WOMAN'S PLACE

Wendy Kremer

Sarah Courtney has lived with her aunt and uncle, a prosperous merchant, since her father died a year ago. When the handsome and wealthy Ross Balfour catches her eye, she has no expectation of marrying him — until they accidentally fall into a compromising situation, and he offers for her hand to save her reputation. Ross's plan is for the union to be a sham so that Sarah can receive her inheritance and fulfil her dream of opening an apothecary's shop. Love will never enter into it . . . or will it?